The Women of Light: Betta's Story

Le Donne della Luce: La Storia di Betta

Also by Laura M. Alberghini Ventimiglia

A Letter to My Children:
An Italian American Family's Heritage

Nonna, What is St. Peter's Fiesta?

A third-generation Italian American whose ancestors are from the region of Emilia Romagna, Laura is married to a Sicilian American and is passionate about their Italian heritage. During her frequent travels to Italy, she visits family, conducts research, and delves deeper into their shared ancestry. She lives in Gloucester, Massachusetts, with her family.

Laura è italo-americana di terza generazione, i suoi antenati provengo dalla regione Emilia Romagna. È sposata con un italo-americano siciliano ed è appassionata delle loro radici italiana. Durante i suoi frequenti viaggi in Italia, visita la famiglia, conduce ricerche e si immerge più a fondo nel loro comune passato. Vive a Gloucester, Massachusetts, con la sua famiglia.

The Women of Light: Betta's Story

Le Donne della Luce: La Storia di Betta

Laura M. Alberghini Ventimiglia

Laura M. Alberghini Ventimiglia

Translated by
Diletta Ballati

Illustrated by
Allie Nicastro

Buttieri Press, LLC
Gloucester, Ma
USA

Library of Congress Control Number: 2025908264
ISBN: 978-0-9976486-2-1

Published by
Buttieri Press, LLC
Gloucester, Massachusetts 01930
buttieripress.com

Edited by
Weber Writing and Research
weberwriting.com

Designed by
Camille Vicenti
camillevicenti.com

Printed in the United States of America

First Edition

To the resilient and courageous women of Terrasini.

Alle donne resilienti e coraggiose di Terrasini.

CONTENTS

INDICE

FAMILY CHART

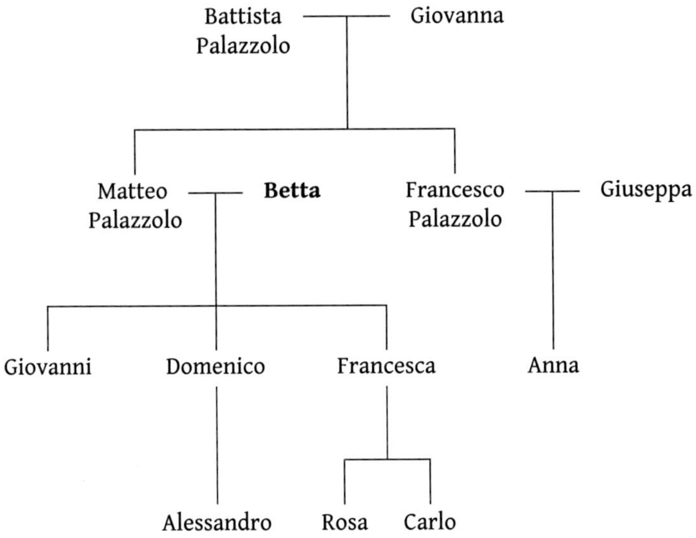

VILLAGE FRIENDS AND CHARACTERS

Maria, Luigi, and their son Nunzio; Grazia and her daughter Caterina; Giulia, Filippo, and their daughter Sara; Vincenza, Enzo, and their son Salvatore; Serafina; Antonina and her daughter Ninfa; Lucrezia; Margherita; Angelina; and Vito, the fruit and vegetable vendor.

The Women of Light:
Betta's Story

It's September 21, 1740, the feast day of Saint Matthew. Matteo has been gone for twelve years. My daughter, Francesca, and I are making pastries for Matteo's *onomastico*, his name day, his Saint's Day, the day we celebrate Saint Matthew whose name Matteo carried.

We always celebrated when Matteo was alive. A big *onomastico* dinner. Back then, my Matteo was tall and thin but rugged with dark olive skin, his thick black hair rested high atop his head, a mustache huddled under his nose. He held the seat of honor at the table with our Palazzolo family squished around it like fish in the nets hauled onto the boats in our fishing village. Our sons, Giovanni and Domenico, were on Matteo's left; I sat at his right near the stove, ready to bring over the next dish. A young Francesca sat next to me, and the table was often graced with a little bouquet of wildflowers she would pick for her father.

The sounds that filled the air were merry, forks clinking in rhythm with voices, interrupted only by bites of food. We feasted on dish after dish of pasta, fish with whatever vegetables Vito, our neighborhood vendor, was selling from his cart at the corner, cheese and fruit, prickly pears were our favorite. Such an indulgence was saved for special occasions in our poor family of fishermen.

At the other end of the table were Nonno Battista, Matteo's father, and Nonna Giovanna, Matteo's mother, who would serve the food as I put it out. Francesco, Matteo's younger brother, was sure to keep the jugs of wine and water filled. Ahh, having drinking water was such a pleasure. Then, like now, we went every day to the public fountain in the piazza where we met our neighbors, chatted, and drew our water, carrying it home in jugs heavy and overflowing. We finished our meal with *una torta di marzapane*, the sweet dessert that was Matteo's favorite. But before we left the table and before Giuseppa, Francesco's wife, helped clean up and Anna, their young daughter, went off giggling and laughing with Francesca, we'd pass around the wine one more time and toast to our Matteo.

Oh, how I remember those days. Oh, how Matteo could melt my heart just looking at him. If only he were still with us. Ahh, Matteo.

To honor him and his life we still celebrate his *onomastico* with pastries: *Cassateddi di Ricotta, Giuggiulena*, and his favorite, *una torta di marzapane*. It helps me feel close to him and keeps his memory alive for our family. While Francesca and I bake today, my grandchildren, Rosa, Carlo, and Alessandro, play at our feet.

"Mamma," Francesca says, "tell the children about the day you saved Nonno Matteo and our village."

Rosa chimes in, "Please, Nonna Betta. I love this story!"

"A story, yeah!" Carlo shouts as he throws up his arms.

Alessandro pulls on my skirt, "Story. Story."

"*Va bene. Venite qui.*" I say to them. "All right. All right. Come here with me."

I settle into the wooden chair in the corner by the window. Its cracked turquoise paint and worn flowered pillow remind me of my wedding day. It was a gift from Matteo's parents welcoming me into their family. Each time I sit there, I feel the embrace of their love and the love of Matteo. The shutters on the window are open to the voices of our neighbors and the bright light of day.

Rosa skips over singing, "*È stata una bella giornata!*" Carlo dances around her. They all laugh knowing what's coming as she continues to sing, "*È stata una bella giornata!*" Carlo climbs on my lap. Rosa settles down and curls up at my feet, holding Alessandro. The sun shines in on their eager faces. A hush falls over the room. I begin as I always do . . .

È stata una bella giornata! It was a beautiful day! It could have been a June day in early summer, but it wasn't. In our tiny fishing village of Terrasini it was Sunday, September 1, 1726. From the balcony outside our bedroom doors, I could see the harbor. I watched the fishing boats sail out to sea, out past *la Torre Mulinazzo*, the stone tower that stands guard against adversaries approaching from the waters along our coast. In the reddish-orange light of dawn reflecting off the ocean, I could make out Matteo's wooden boat among the others, its bold royal-blue trim painted above the bright colors of orange, white, and *ocra gialla*. While he rowed, the mast and its sail rested next to him along the starboard side. His routine was familiar. Outside the harbor he'd step the mast and draw the sail.

I waved. I knew Matteo could not see me, or could he? On this day, Sunday, our sacred time together each week, was he looking longingly at our house, regretting his absence from our family? He would be home were it not for the poverty of our village and the abundance of fish in our waters.

Yes, I remember that beautiful day with the bright morning sunlight filling the cloudless blue sky. The peacefulness of it all. Yet I began waving frantically, wishing him to see me. A burning sensation surged through my body. What was it I wondered? What was the urgency to wave, for him to see me as if it could be the last time? I chastised myself. Betta, stop being so emotional. Matteo will be fine.

His fishing boat, along with the others, was now out of view. I waved one last time, wistfully, not wanting to let go. As I turned back into our bedroom a chill crept through my body. Despite the early morning heat, I shivered.

I tiptoed through the kitchen to the back bedroom. It was too early to wake the children, but I needed to see them. Gently I opened the creaky door to peek at 8-year-old Francesca. Her rag doll cuddled in her arms, her wavy brown hair a delicate fan on her pillow, Francesca was smiling as if the angels were telling her a wonderful story while she slept. I pulled back the curtain separating her from the boys and looked in. They were sleeping soundly. Domenico, an 11-year-old wild cat, was all tangled up in his bed-clothes. Giovanni, at 15 years old, tall and strong like his father, would have been out fishing with him. But, as Matteo was slipping out of bed in the early morning darkness he whispered, "Betta, let the boy sleep. He can stay home today and help you."

I turned back into the kitchen, grateful for Matteo's love for our family. The sun showed its brilliance as a path to the heavens streaming in through the wooden slats on the double doors. I threw them open. The bright light flowed in and raised my spirit while filling every corner of the room with its energy. The swirling light carried my prayer for Matteo's safety around the room, out the door, and up to our Heavenly Father. The warming protection of the sunny day enveloped me. I started to sing softly and danced around the table. I was preparing a treat for breakfast of warm, freshly made bread smothered in olive oil flavored with rosemary and other herbs I gathered from the dry, cracked earth further up the mountain near the outskirts of town. *È stata una bella giornata!*

A rustling behind me told of children waking. They tumbled into the kitchen—one by one—yawning, rubbing eyes, stretching arms high toward the ceiling. Laughing at my cheerfulness, they joined in my dance. Around and around we went. Domenico pulled Francesca's hair. Her squeals delighted him. She reached for his bouncing black curls and missed. Giggling and poking each other, they collapsed into their seats at the table.

The beauty of that day stretched its reach to our family. Domenico and Francesca played merrily without the usual squabbling over this or that, without the pushing or shoving that often ended with one or the other bumping into the table and teeter-tottering it to near collapse, without the morning's milk spilling drip, drip, drip to the floor, without food flying through the air and out the balcony doors feeding breakfast to the lazy dog who sleeps all day in the sun of the *Piazza Duomo.*

We settled around the table laughing and chatting, happy to be together but missing Matteo terribly. Talking about Matteo helped us feel like he was with us, so we made plans for when he would arrive home. Suddenly the musical bells of *la Chiesa di Santa Rosalia* started to ring, signaling the day had begun. "Shoo! Shoo!" I said, "Quickly, clean up and get ready for church. *Andiamo!*"

Going down the stairs from our home we greeted Giuseppa and Anna in the hallway. Francesco was out fishing too. We all lived together in the house of Nonno Battista and Nonna Giovanna. Francesco and his family lived with them on the first floor, we lived in the rooms upstairs.

"Nonna Giovanna and Nonno Battista aren't ready," said Giuseppa. "We have to wait."

Giuseppa was my friend. We shared a bond of sisterhood, living in the same house, caring for each other's families and our husbands' parents. Giuseppa was the cautious younger woman in our household and looked to me for strength and guidance. For me, Giuseppa was my trusted confidante. I could always share my ideas, thoughts, or opinions and I could count on her honesty and support whenever I needed it.

We stood just outside the front door and waited for Nonno Battista and Nonna Giovanna while waving and calling out to our neighbors as they passed by on their way to church, "*Buon giorno! Buon giorno! Buona domenica!*"

Giuseppa and I each took an arm of Nonna and Nonno. Slowly we walked up the hill of our mountain-side village. Feeling the heat of that beautiful day, we worked our way up its steep slope. *La Chiesa di Santa Rosalia*, standing tall at the crest of our neighborhood, rang her bells again. Mass was about to begin. The children ran ahead. Once more, Domenico started teasing Francesca, this time jumping around her and making foolish faces. Giovanni stepped in like his father and I heard him say, "Domenico, *basta*! Enough! Leave

Francesca alone. Pay attention." I smiled, pleased that our family was together.

We reached the steps of *la Chiesa di Santa Rosalia* with her tall wooden carved doors. Just as I entered, I heard a whisper in my ear, "*Betta, Oh Betta.*" I turned towards it and saw only the distant light blue ocean glorious under the clear sky and shining sun. Goosebumps rose on my skin and chills crawled up my spine. What was happening? In the blur of the moment, I saw Matteo. He was fine. Strong and focused on his work, his muscles bulging, he was pulling a net full of fish over the side of his boat. I shook it off.

Inside, the white stone walls kept the air comfortable and refreshing, offering relief from the oppressive heat outside. The singing voices of our neighbors greeted us. The sculptured statue of the *Madonna del Rosario* holding a child on her lap in the niche above the altar welcomed us. Saintly images on canvas stood watch over us. A statue of *San Pietro*, the patron saint of fishermen, stood tall in his own niche. I looked at Matteo's miniature boat that hung, along with others from fishing families, below the statue of *San Pietro*. I prayed for his safety out at sea, as I always do. When we were first married, Matteo carved this boat, painted it like his own, and gave it to me to hold him close when he was out fishing. I brought it here to our church and hung it as an offering. In devotion to *San Pietro* and our God, I offered this tiny boat in thanks for their constant protection of Matteo. Thinking of Matteo and picturing him as I just did, with a net full of fish, a smile flickered across my lips and a rush of affection filled my heart.

Don Paolo, virtuous in his devotion, entered from the sacristy his voice joining ours in jubilation. Our worship began. I sat on our bench, relaxed, knowing I was blessed. I knew that faith was the soul of the village, and our families, its heart. We needed no reminder of the fury to be thrust upon us, of divine punishment should we not obey our Lord, for all we did then and continue to do, we do willingly in service to God and our neighbors. We watched over each other and the children of our village. When the fish were scarce, we fed one another's family; when birthdays were upon us, we gathered together; when a child or wife or husband was sick, we took care of them; when good fortune landed at one family's doorstep, we rejoiced. And why not? Upon *i faraglioni*, the rock formations gracing the water's edge, the ocean, the grottos, and the mountains surrounding our village, we knew our God stood Almighty, embracing us in his protection. Together we celebrated our good fortunes. Together, helping each other, we faced our poverty and challenges. On that day we were secure in our happiness. We were protected from the world outside, snug in our little town built into the basin at the bottom of our mountains, the mountains that kept the world from intruding upon us.

Mass came to an end. Released into the scorching heat of the day, we left *Santa Rosalia*. Drawn to the beach by its tranquil, cooling water, we walked back down the hill faster than we climbed, the earth pulling our feet down, down, down. We arrived at our front door just a few houses from the cliff that drops into the sea. A splendid sight greeted us, the glistening light blue water of the distant deep ocean peeking out beyond the staggering rocks overgrown with tuffs of wild grass and flowers. In my mind's eye I saw Matteo. He was out there, somewhere, fishing for us. His love reached back to me. A long deep breath swelled in my chest and escaped through my mouth. Ahhh, a beautiful moment on that beautiful day.

Nonna and Nonno went inside for *un riposo.* Giuseppa, the children and I kept walking to the steep winding path that took us down through the craggy rocks to the fine brown sand of our beach. We were lucky that the dusty, oppressive winds of the *Scirocco* were not upon us. It was a perfect day as summer came to a close. The crystal-clear water in patches of deep blue and turquoise green glided in towards the beach over the rippled sandy ocean floor and swirled around *i faraglioni.* The sun's rays reached down through a cloudless sky and sparkles flickered on the water's surface. Francesca and Anna ran to the water's edge dancing and splashing around. The boys dove in, clothes sticking to their skin, they swam and dived like giant fish. The premonitions of the morning forgotten in the beauty and peacefulness of the day, I sat with Giuseppa on the sand.

Giuseppa, a note of concern in her voice, said, "I worry more and more about Nonna Giovanna and Nonno Battista. They get tired easily and they seem so frail."

"I noticed it too and it must be difficult living in the same rooms with them and caring for them when they need help, yet without making them feel dependent on you, without making them feel old and decrepit."

"It is," Giuseppa sighed. "I know you are upstairs to help, but I feel so bad for them. They've always been so vibrant."

"What if we start having our family gatherings in your home so they don't have to climb the stairs to our house?"

"That would be wonderful. Thanks."

"And I'll do more to help downstairs."

Our chatter turned casual. We let the warmth of the sun flow down on us and watched the frolicking of our children. We knew in our hearts that our riches flowed from the love of our families and the safety of our beautiful, small town.

Carlo jumps up and down on my lap, clapping his hands. "Nonna, after this story can we go to the beach?"

"Hmmm, that does sound like fun."

"Shh," says Rosa, "I want to hear Nonna Betta's story and now Alessandro is all in a fuss."

"But I wanna go to the beach. I like it when we go to the beach. Nonna, I can show you how I can swim. Please?"

"Remember we are having an *onomastico* party for Nonno Matteo?"

"But after I swim we can dig in the sand, and you can help me make a fort. I bet Alessandro wants to build a fort too. Please? Please?"

"*Va bene*, we'll go to the beach after we celebrate Nonno Matteo. Now, back to the story."

The floor moved. Or did it? My back to the open kitchen door I was bent over the table in the middle of the room rolling out the dough for our dinner of *pasta con le sarde*. We decided to surprise Matteo with a feast upon his return home to celebrate that glorious day and let him know how much we missed him. Matteo's favorite, sardines, were almost always in his net. I was sure we could count on them for our table that night. Thc sweet aroma of anise from the wild fennel I chopped earlier filled the air. Later I would blend it with the tanginess of sardines and fry them together ever so lightly in olive oil.

I brushed wisps of hair off my forehead and dreamt of Matteo. Suddenly I was blinded by a smothering darkness that had crept in behind me through the open doors. My heart stopped. Then it jolted back to life beating faster and faster. What was happening?

The floor shook again. A slight tremor, barely noticeable, but this time I was certain. I heard the broom in the corner tap the wall in rhythm to the dishes that were surely dancing as they rattled against each other on their shelves. I stood, alert. Far, far away I heard a low rumbling noise.

I turned slightly, leaning against the table, and faced the blackness. I heard screams piercing in from outside. Nothing like this had ever happened. What was this assault on our village?

Oh Mio Dio! The children. Where were the children? I screamed for them. "Francesca! Domenico! Giovanni!" No answer. The rolling pin dropped from my hands with a bang. Flour flew up in the air, hitting me in my face and spreading its dust. Giovanni was going to the *piazzetta* to gather drinking water from the public fountain for dinner. Maybe he took Domenico and Francesca with him. I screamed for Giuseppa. No answer. Where was she? Where was Anna? Where were Nonno Battista and Nonna Giovanna? Feeling my way, I stumbled down the flight of stairs unable to see where I was going. I screamed out their names the whole way. "Francesca! Domenico! Giovanni! Giuseppa! Anna! Nonno! Nonna!"

People poured out of their homes. Cries. Shouts. Chaos. I tried to run through the crowd, my long skirt gathered in my right hand, I used my left hand to guide me. It was pitch black. Our sunny afternoon had disappeared, swallowed up by what appeared to be one giant black raging cloud. I could only see where I was going when I was there, one step at a time. My feet slipped on the pebbles in the dirt. The bells of *la Chiesa di Santa Rosalia* tolled loudly sending out an alarm so fast and loud that the harsh metallic blast thundered in my ears. I headed towards our church and the *Piazzetta Santa Rosalia*, hoping my children were there.

One foot in front of the other I forced myself up the hill. Panting as I ran, the air rushed in attacking my lungs and burning them with each breath. My heart was pounding. I held my chest to ease the pain.

Where were my children? Where was our family? What was happening to our village? The menacing darkness was more terrifying than anything I had ever imagined. The giant black cloud lowered itself around us and tightened its grip on the whole town. And why did the ground continue to shift but ever so slightly? *Per favore Cara Santa Rosalia*, protect my children! Protect our children! Protect our village! *Cara Maria Santissima delle Grazie, prega per noi,* pray for us.

I heard the familiar voice of Giuseppa screaming for Anna. "Giuseppa," I shouted.

"Betta," Giuseppa yelled, "have you seen Anna?"

"No. Where are Nonna Giovanna and Nonno Battista?"

"They are fine, in the house but scared. I told them to stay there, stay close to each other, and not move."

Neighbors were yelling to each other. I heard friends call my name. "Betta, what will we do?" hollered Antonina. "Betta, I'm frightened for my Salvatore," Vincenza called out, "Can you help me find him?" "Betta," shouted Maria, "I don't know where my little Nunzio went to play."

The pain in my lungs and heart did not stop me in my race against time to find my children but for one quick second. I bent over, hands on knees to give my body a rest. It was only a second, though. The crowd of mothers looking for their children pushed me on. Surrounded by a thick haze of fear, we raced together in our frantic search.

I screamed, or tried to scream, but the words came out in a whisper, "Francesca, Domenico, Giovanni, where are you?"

I took longer strides up the hill, breathing heavier and slipping as I went. My hips, pulled apart by the longer steps carrying me up, up, up, joined the pain in my chest. This climb to our *Chiesa di Santa Rosalia* and her *piazzetta* seemed steeper than I ever remembered.

I wanted to stop again but I couldn't. I was almost there and I wasn't alone. The swarm of mothers carried me along. In the darkness, we bumped into each other, tripping as we went, but we kept on. Our voices fought to be heard over one another and the church bells as we shouted for our sons and daughters.

The buzzing in my ears collided with the screams in my head. My children, my children where are you? I tried to yell to them again, "Francesca, Domenico, Giovanni," but their names stuck in the dryness of my mouth, dried out by the air gushing in on its way to my burning lungs. *Per favore, per favore Caro Gesù,* please, please dear Jesus, protect my children. *Cara Maria Santissima delle Grazie, prega per noi,* pray for us, pray for us. Could God even hear my prayers over the hammering of my heart and the buzzing in my ears? Was it even possible for my silent prayers to reach the heavenly world?

I reached the *piazzetta.* I heard a rumble of voices and recognized Giovanni's. My voice rose against the pain in my body, against the church bells, against the other voices, and I screamed louder and louder, "Giovanni! Giovanni!" Again and again, I screamed. He heard me and followed my voice till I felt a hug. *Grazie Santa Rosalia. Grazie mille Caro Gesù. Grazie Cara Madre Maria.* He was safe and with him was Domenico who clung to my waist. Jostled by the other mothers running past, we hugged each other tightly murmuring our love and thankfulness to have found each other. But where was Francesca? Where are you my poor frightened little girl?

Clinging to each other so we wouldn't get separated, we worked our way back towards the house, pushing gently through the crush of panicked mothers. We kept screaming, "Francesca! Francesca! Francesca!"

We checked all her favorite hiding spots. We asked her friends' families, "Have you seen our Francesca? Francesca Palazzolo?" Nothing. *Niente.* Oh no! The beach and the harbor. She never goes there alone but did she get turned around? Confused? *Oh Mio Dio, Oh Santa Madre Maria,* could she have ended up in the water?

We reached our house. Nonna Giovanna and Nonno Battista were standing frozen in the doorway. "Giovanni," I pleaded, "run upstairs and search the house for Francesca. Domenico and I will stay here and look after your *Nonni* to be sure they are all right."

I heard him bumbling up the stairs into the murky nothingness, crying out, "Francesca! Francesca! Francesca, are you here?" Then he was gone.

Enveloped by the blackness and the noise of the crowd, my heart pounded as if it would burst any moment. A buzzing still hammered my ears. Cries of frightened babies came from open windows. Rustling skirts and feet pushed by. Panicked mothers shouted for their children—Sara, Caterina, Ninfa—where are you? I hugged Nonna Giovanna and stroked Nonno Battista's shoulder. They were trembling. I switched. I hugged Nonno and held Nonna's hand. All the while I was silently praying. Please, please God, let Francesca be safe. *Santa Madre Maria prega per Francesca, prega per noi.*

Then I heard it. A tiny whimpering voice getting closer and closer. "Mamma. Mamma."

Giovanni found her! He found Anna too. Exhausted from an afternoon of cousins playing with each other, they had fallen asleep snuggled together on Anna's bed. A scared girl in each arm, Giovanni emerged. At the same time, Giuseppa arrived at the house running up from the beach. She had gone searching there for Anna.

Together again, we huddled in the doorway. Gradually overcoming our shock, gradually trusting we would be okay, we relaxed enough to hug, kiss and comfort each other, over and over again. We began to think and wonder aloud what happened? The big black cloud still blanketed us, but we had found each other and were together again. The neighborhood started to quiet down as families were reunited. We were safe. Exhausted, we went inside.

"Giovanni," I said, "we need to get some light in here. Let's light the candles we save for special times."

"But Mamma," he replied, "they are too expensive. They cost too much money, and we only have a few of them. Why don't we use the *lucerne*, our oil lamps instead?"

"No, Giovanni. Your brother and sister need to know that we'll be all right. The candles will let them know everything is okay." To myself I said, *Grazie, Dio Mio, Grazie Santa Rosalia, Grazie Maria Santissima delle Grazie,* for the safety of my family.

Still not knowing what hit our little village, I quickly checked our home. With only the glow bouncing off the children's candle as they huddled around it at the kitchen table in the room where we spent our days, I felt my way around. Downstairs I knew Giuseppa was doing the same. We hollered to each other, "*Va tutto bene.*"

Taking a deep calming breath, I leaned against the doorframe of the open kitchen doors, arms crossed hugging myself. Afraid to step out on the balcony, I looked out into the black abyss of the cloud that still choked our village. The silence roared back at me. The birds weren't chattering. The streets were empty of its sounds. The bushes and woody undergrowth of the cliffs weren't rustling. Quick, shallow breaths started to bubble up. Gasping for air, my heart pounded. I pressed on my chest to keep from choking, to force my breathing back to the calm I felt seconds earlier, but my fear pushed through.

Matteo! What was happening to him out on the ocean? The blackness extended as far as I could see. It obscured the view of the sky and the land. The specks of candle lights burning in our homes that could lead the way to our village were hidden by the raging black cloud. Without those flickers from shore, without the fading light of day, how would he, how would any of the fishermen find their way back home? How would they find the harbor and avoid crashing into the peninsula where *la Torre Mulinazzo* or *i faraglioni* sit along the coast? They should be here by now!

I yelled to the children, "Stay here." I flew past them and ran down the stairs. I had an idea. *Caro Gesù, Cara Santa Rosalia, Cara Santa Madre Maria* please let it work. Beating on the door of Nonno and Nonna I screamed, "Open up, open up, we have to help our men!" Giuseppa threw open the door, "*Madonna mia!*" she exclaimed.

I shared my plan with Giuseppa and we took it to the women of our village. We ran into the street hollering, calling to our neighbors. "Maria! Grazia! Giulia! Vincenza! Serafina! Antonina! *Tutte le donne* come quick!" Up and down the street we hollered, our voices louder and louder, facing first one side of the street then the other. Back and forth, up and down. The women poured out and gathered closely around us. Gripped in fear, my heart pounding, I shouted, "We must help the fishermen! Listen . . ."

"Betta," said Lucrezia, "I don't know. I'm afraid and it could be dangerous."

Giuseppa jumped in, "It's brilliant. And think about our men out there at sea. It's more dangerous for them. Betta, I'm with you. Who else will help?"

Soft murmurs buzzed among the women. I waited impatiently, arms crossed, tapping my foot. Time was passing and I hoped we weren't already too late. Finally, I heard voices shouting, "Yes! Yes! We will help. We'll do it."

We spread the word from neighborhood to neighborhood, to our *Chiesa di Santa Rosalia* and beyond, with a plan to help our men find their way home.

"Nonna, I'm scared!" Carlo cries out.

"It was scary. I was terrified. But I knew I had to be strong for Francesca, your mother, who was a little girl then, and your uncles Domenico and Giovanni, for Nonno Matteo, and for our whole village."

"I don't like that part of the story," Carlo moaned.

"It was frightening but I also believed that our God, *Maria Santissima delle Grazie,* and *Santa Rosalia* would take care of us."

Rosa reaches up and holds Carlo's hand while Alessandro cuddles on her lap. "Carlo, shhh, this is the best part of the story. Listen."

"Nonna, what happened?" Carlo whispers.

In the darkness, the women of our village split into two groups. Giuseppa and I would take one group to the beach. Maria and Grazia would take the other to the cliff, 100 feet above us. I worried about them. They had the more dangerous route to take. Just getting to the edge of the cliff would be a difficult walk over rocks, crevices, plants, pebbles, and dirt. Once there they would face the same jagged footing plus the danger of getting too close to the edge and its sudden drop. All of this perilous in the light of day, deadly within the gloom that held us captive in its terror. But Maria and Grazia insisted, knowing it was what our men needed. We hugged, letting our hearts talk for us. There was no need for words. Determined, we went our separate ways guided sparingly by tiny flickers of light from a few of our *lucerne.*

Giuseppa and I slowly found our way to the beach down the steep winding footpath worn smooth from years of use. In the dark, we all took tiny steps, feeling our way, children clutching the hands of their mothers, older sisters or brothers, or the strongest of *Nonni* who came with us, determined to help. This was the very beach that Giuseppa and I enjoyed earlier that day with our children. I recalled the girls playing near the water's edge and the boys swimming and diving like giant fish. I remembered the feeling of security, feeling safe in the love of our families nestled in our little village at the base of our mountains protected from the world. I didn't know that we'd be back at the beach amid a frightening and mysterious darkness. I didn't know that the peacefulness of our village would be shattered and our world turned upside down. I didn't know that we would have to save the fishermen of our Terrasini. My heart skipped a beat, then another and another. My breathing quickened. I gasped to control it while my body quivered. My hands trembled. My mind raced. What if the plan doesn't work?

Then I remembered that day's morning Mass and the sense of security that warmed my soul as I sat on the bench in church singing our prayers. I remembered where that feeling came from, from knowing that together, families and neighbors, we face our challenges and good fortunes as one. That together, we help each other, and we stay strong in our faith because we know our God stands as the Almighty, embracing us in His protection. My breathing slowed, my hands steadied, my mind focused. Standing straight, shoulders back, chest surging with confidence, I stepped to the front of the crowd and shouted, repeating the plan to bring our men home. I knew that, rooted in devotion to our God and saints, we were capable of the task at hand.

Dressed in black we blended into the thick darkness of the smothering cloud that locked us in its grip. The ocean waves crashed along the shore. We couldn't see them, but we could hear the turbulent waters. They roared like they were pushing in from beyond *la Torre Mulinazzo*, twirling and spinning, coming in fast and crashing the shore in a fury. Something was happening under the water. Something we could not see but could sense its violence. Yet the salty air was still and cool, the heat of the day chilled by the darkness surrounding us. There had never been a time like this when the waters were stormy while the air was quiet. In the eeriness, my blood ran cold, and a sense of dread rushed over me.

The wet, sticky sand, cold without the glare of the sun, clung to the bottoms of our clothes. Dragged on the clammy sand, they became soggy along with the soles of our shoes, the moisture seeping towards our feet.

The bells of *Santa Rosalia* pealed the location of our village. The fishermen would surely recognize the sound of her two bells hanging next to each other—one large and one small—housed in the tower that sits snugly at the edge of her roof. Pulled by their long ropes, the bell ringers sent their message in a sequence of high and low-pitched sounds out to sea to guide the men towards the shore of their beloved Terrasini.

Armed with our *lucerne* of terracotta in all sizes that we carried from our homes, along with olive oil for fuel and strips of cloth for wicks, we were determined to bring our men home. We knew that by preparing the *lucerne* differently than for lighting our homes, we could create a larger, longer-lasting flame. We also knew that the flames would reflect off our clothes making the light of the fires more visible within the black cloud.

Using the few *lucerne* already lit, we grouped together and worked in silence to get ready. Kneeling on the damp sand we bent over the *lucerne*. Our hands moved quickly, steadily focused on the importance of our task while we sent our prayers up to the heavens. *Cara Maria Santissima delle Grazie, prega per i nostri uomini, prega per noi.* For each *lucerna*, instead of pulling a wick through the hole in its cover, we took all the covers off and left them off. We used long strips of cloth for wicks and curled it around and around, piling it up in the bottom of the *lucerne* till it was sitting out of the bowl, then we filled them with the oil.

When we were ready, everyone lined up side-by-side, shoulder to shoulder, with the very young sitting or lying at the feet of their mothers or their *Nonni*. In open hands, cupped together, everyone held their *lucerna*. Giulia at one end, Angelina at the other, Giuseppa and I in the center, with Margherita, Vincenza, Serafina, and Antonina, their *lucerne* already lit and guiding our work, we walked along and started lighting all the others. I hoped Maria and Grazia were doing the same high above us. *Per favore Santa Rosalia. Per favore Madre Maria*, they made it safely to the cliff.

Holding our fire steels in one hand bound around our fingers and over our knuckles, we struck them with our flints. The hot sparks dropped onto the wicks. As they landed, each person worked steadily to light their *lucerna*, blowing gently on the sparks, over and over again, to fully ignite the flame. We lit our own, joined the linc, and we were ready.

In the stillness of the night but with the noise of the furious waves crashing and churning, we created one continuous blazing flame along the curved length of the beach. High above, along the cliff, another continuous flame matching ours appeared. *Oh Mio Dio, grazie. Grazie Santa Rosalia. Grazie Madre Maria.* The fires burned upwards to the sky illuminating the coast of our Terrasini. We became our own sea of light to guide our men home, the landmark they needed to find their way safely into the harbor.

Our collective breaths were held silent in prayer. Please let this work. *Grazie Caro Gesù*, thank you, dear Jesus, for carrying our light out to sea, for shining our light bright enough to be seen. *Cara Santa Rosalia, Cara Madre Maria, per favore*, bring our men home safely. *Cara Maria Santissima delle Grazie, prega per i nostri uomini, prega per noi, prega per nostro paese.*

The bells of *Santa Rosalia* continued to ring out. Loud and steady in their message. Forcing their signal out over the turbulent waters.

We waited and waited. We listened. Silent. Vigilant. Arms out straight, the flames of our *lucerne* grew, the glow of the flames warmed our faces. We sent our prayers outward and upward for our husbands, fathers, brothers, sons, uncles to return safely. Confident in our men's abilities, we waited patiently. Confident in our God, we prayed. We held back our fears, knowing, hoping that soon our families and village would once again be whole.

We waited with our fires burning brightly against our black clothes in the darkest of times. We waited some more. Our silent prayers found a harmonious voice. First in a whisper, then louder and louder, our voices lifted together to the heavens. *Cara Maria Santissima delle Grazie, prega per i nostri uomini, prega per noi, prega per nostro paese. Cara Maria Santissima delle Grazie, prega per i nostri uomini, prega per noi, prega per nostro paese. Cara Maria Santissima delle Grazie, prega per i nostri uomini, prega per noi, prega per nostro paese.* The church bells rang and rang.

Then we heard it. The faint but steady rhythmic swishing of oars moving towards us. We listened to be sure, to be sure that our ears were not tricking us. But the splash of the oars grew louder. From the beach and the cliff, our voices shouted out for joy.

Each screaming our own loved one's name. Matteo! Francesco! Luigi! Enzo! Filippo! All the names roared into the air. Our voices colliding with each other. The children ran along the edge of the water, jumping, waving their arms, screaming, their excitement visible in the glow of our fires. I heard the loud voices of Francesca and Anna. "*Papà! Papà! Papà!*" Suddenly a babel of shouts erupted. Hooray! Yay! *Grazie Madre Maria!* Here they are! They made it! *Mille grazie Santa Rosalia!* Hallelujah! *Oh Mio Dio, grazie!*

At last, our men came into view. Through the blaze that billowed in front of us, we watched them get closer and closer. Straining their bodies, back, forward, back, the pull of arms on the oars, in and out of the water. The wild waves of the ocean parting as they pulled themselves home. Closer and closer. Closer still. In the brightness of our collective flame, we saw them. We saw the fishing boats. We saw our husbands, fathers, sons, brothers, and uncles. I saw my Matteo.

"Yay," Carlo shouts, "everyone is safe."

"I told you it was the best part," said Rosa, "and Nonna Betta you were so smart to think of a plan, and all the women, too, who helped the men come home, right?"

"Yes, we were smart, and we were all very brave."

"Nonna, you were afraid, and you still helped the fishermen," said Carlo. "Was my mother afraid too?"

Francesca looked over from the stove where she was baking, "Carlo, I was a little girl. I was afraid at first, but Nonna Betta and all the women were so strong they took care of us too. They made sure we were safe. And Giovanni, your uncle, stayed the whole time with me, your Uncle Domenico, my cousin Anna, and our *Nonni*, your great-grandparents. He didn't leave us at all. Nonna knew she could trust him to keep us safe."

"Wow, Nonna," Carlo said, "I'm glad I wasn't there. I would have really been afraid."

"I'm sure you would have been a brave little boy." Smiling at my grandchildren, I whisper, "Oh, look,

Alessandro is asleep. Let's finish the story and have our party for Nonno Matteo."

The day was done. The big black cloud was gone. Calm settled in. The entire town rested in the safety of its families, in their homes, snuggled in the coziness of their beds. I lay in Matteo's arms while he held me tightly. I felt his love and exhaustion. As he nodded off to sleep, I heard him whisper, "Thank you for saving me today, Betta. Thank you for saving all of us. Thank you for saving our village. *Sei meravigliosa.*"

Lying there I looked out the open double doors extending to our balcony. I couldn't sleep. Thinking of the day we had survived, my body shuddered from the chilling memory. I recalled the omens of the morning. Had Matteo sensed it too, leaving Giovanni home to help with our family? *Madonna mia!*

Getting up quietly so as not to wake Matteo or anyone in the house, I tiptoed to the doors. Still afraid to walk on the balcony I looked out over the ocean and up. Only the darkness of night remained but, it was a hopeful sky full of stars shining brightly. A sky that once again connected us with our families, our friends, our village, and to God and His universe. The bright crescent moon shined upon us. The stars twinkled their message, led by the brightest star of all, "You were steadfast in your faith, and you are safe." In gratitude, I looked in the direction of our church, our *Chiesa di Santa Rosalia*. It was then that I saw a light below in the street. Was it my friend Maria in her doorway?

I wrapped my shawl around my shoulders and slipped out of the bedroom. As I passed through the kitchen, I picked up the candle that gave light to our home earlier in the day. Carefully, I made my way down the stairs, hugging the wall as I went, shaken from the day's events but freed from its terror, glad it was over. I opened the front door to the street. I saw Maria, the flame of her candle lighting her up.

Then Grazia and Giulia, Vincenza, Serafina, Antonina, Lucrezia. Soon I saw others too.

I stood in the doorway, holding my candle, looking up the street toward our *Chiesa di Santa Rosalia*. Imagining that brightest star lighting up the sacred cross on the peak of her roof, I offered thanks to her, the patron saint of our region, for protecting us. Gazing at the sky I thanked God and the saints for saving our men. I thanked *Maria Santissima delle Grazie* for interceding on our behalf and saving our whole community from the havoc of the day. One by one, other doors rippled open on the narrow houses attached one to the other leading to our *Santa Rosalia*. Families poured out with their own light of thanks.

The stairs creaked behind me, muffled footsteps, four pairs of them climbed down slowly. Nestled in each other's arms, Matteo and I stood with our children as one. Giuseppa and her family joined us. Our village, neighborhoods, and families were together once again.

The flood of candle lights moved up the street, bouncing off the earth-toned colors of our homes, lighting the way up our mountain towards *la Chiesa di Santa Rosalia.*

Suddenly her bells began to ring. Their musical sound grew louder and louder filling our ears with their joyfulness. Soothing our souls at the end of a tortuous yet triumphant day. They sang to us for a whole hour swaddling us once more in the safety of our faith. The bells of *Santa Rosalia* sounded till midnight when they rang in the new day. A day to thank God for creating light, for giving us the wisdom to use it through the illumination of fire, for the men to see it and return home; a day to once again be in the security of our tiny village at the foot of our mountains.

As I stood there listening to the church bells, safe again, I thought, forever we will remember this time. We will pass its story along to our children and grandchildren. They will pass it to their children and grandchildren, down through the generations so that in hundreds and hundreds of years people will still know that the women of Terrasini saved their fishing village from the plunder of darkness.

"Thank you, Nonna Betta," Rosa exclaims. "This is my favorite story. I promise to tell it to my children and grandchildren."

Carlo chimes in, "Me too, me too, Nonna. Now that I know how it ends, I love this story."

Rosa pokes him, "Yes, Nonna, we'll keep your story alive."

Francesca looks at me and smiles. A knowing smile remembering that day and touched by her daughter's eagerness to carry on our storytelling tradition.

We are in our kitchen on the ground floor in the same house where we lived on that frightening day. Nonno Battista and Nonna Giovanna have passed on, and the house now belongs to us. Francesca and her family live with me. Domenico and his family live upstairs, yet Alessandro is always here playing with his cousins.

"The pastries are ready," Francesca calls out.

I watch the children as they run off to get their treat. My heart heavy with the danger of that day but warmed by the memories of Matteo and our family, I whisper, *Buon Onomastico, Matteo, Buon Onomastico!*

POSTSCRIPT

This story was inspired by the brave women of Terrasini, Sicily, as told in a legend passed down through generations. On September 1, 1726, an unusual meteorological event struck their tiny village, and the legend tells of the women's vital role in its aftermath. I was fortunate to hear it directly from Vincenza Randazzo.

I met Vincenza in January 2020 when she was a staff member at the *Biblioteca e Archivio Storico*, the Library and Historical Archives, in Terrasini. With a shrug, she said, "No one ever writes about the women." The tradition of oral storytelling is how she, and many others, preserved these histories.

With Vincenza's words ringing in my ears, I felt inspired to honor the women and other villagers who helped bring the fishermen home that day. For me, and for many, passing down stories through the spoken word is more than mere entertainment. Sometimes it is the only history we know of our families and communities. While some details may be missing or yet to be discovered, I have taken creative license to retell the story.

A Meteorological Event

Uncertainty exists around the details of this event in Terrasini, but in nearby Palermo on September 1, 1726, at five minutes to four in the morning, an earthquake battered the city. A blazing fire followed, ravaging its center, killing hundreds, destroying buildings, and creating mayhem.

The effects of that earthquake in Palermo are probably what struck Terrasini, which could have happened simultaneously but, according to some current stories and traditions, are also likely to have been an aftereffect. My story presupposes the incident occurred in the afternoon.

The Birth of New Traditions

The powerful experience of this event gave rise to a tradition. On the night of each subsequent September 1, before midnight, families gathered in their doorways as they had on that fateful day. Illuminated by the light of their flickering candles, they prayed in thanksgiving for their safety and escape from danger. Church bells robustly filled the air in remembrance, until the new day arrived at 12 AM.

In 2016, the year of the 290th anniversary of this event, the municipality of Terrasini published a booklet, *A Terrasini il 1 settembre acccade che . . .* , commemorating the tradition and explaining its history as recounted by Salvatore Cascio.

The writings of Salvatore Cascio, once Director of the *Biblioteca,* include excerpts from the diary of D. Antonino Mongitore from 1720 to 1736, and offer a glimpse of reported accounts describing the September 1, 1726 event. Later stories as told to Don Raffaele Speciale in the early years of his service at the parish of *Maria SS. delle Grazie,* also included in the writings of Salvatore Cascio, offer contradictory memories so that the exact phenomenon that occurred to create this tradition in Terrasini is unknown: earthquake, tidal wave, or black cloud.

Don Raffaele Speciale embraced the tradition of September 1. He established a liturgical program to honor it because, as reported by Salvatore Cascio, Don Raffaele Speciale believed a deeper, more significant spiritual celebration was appropriate. He embedded the celebration within the Feast of the *Madonna delle Grazie*, now recognized as the Patron Saint of Terrasini, and is widely credited with intervening on behalf of the villagers and saving their town on that fateful September 1, 1726.

Known as the "*Notte delle Luci*," the "Night of Lights," the tradition of families gathering in their doorways surrounded by candles and lanterns also continues and has grown to include bright lights erected in the *Piazza Duomo* in front of the Mother Church, *Maria SS. delle Grazie*.

Other stories of heroism abound like that of September 1, 1726. Within the past century, women of Terrasini have been known to line the harbor with lights to help their fishermen return safely home. Maria (Mia) Millefoglie, a native of Gloucester, Massachusetts, and frequent visitor to Terrasini, learned from one of her Sicilian cousins of a time in the 1930s when Mia's great-grandfather, Antonio Millefoglie, was in a storm and her great-grandmother, Antonia Cracchiolo, was one of the women in the port holding a large pillar candle. As the story goes, the women also took a framed portrait of the Madonna to the port with them, a painting that hangs in *la Chiesa di Maria Ss. Della Provvidenza.*

Betta and Matteo's Family

The names of the family members depicted in this story are real. In 1726 Paola Elisabetta L'Abbate (known as *Betta* in this story) and her family lived in Cinisi. (Cinisi included Favarotta, the fishing village later known as Terrasini.) The family consisted of Paola, her husband Matteo Palazzolo and their three children: Giovanni, Domenico, and Francesca; Matteo's brother, Francesco Palazzolo, his wife Antonina Giuseppa Cavataio and their daughter Anna; the parents of Matteo and Francesco, Giambattista Palazzolo and Giovanna Giordano. Giambattista and Giovanna had several other children but they do not appear in this story. Rosa, Carlo, and Alessandro were the grandchildren of Paola. Recognizing that information today about family histories of centuries past cannot always be taken literally, Rosa is portrayed as 6 years old, Carlo is 5, and Alessandro is 2.

Betta's Family and Connection to Gloucester, Massachusetts, USA

With the abundance of fish along Terrasini's coast, scores of fishermen began settling there in the 17th century. While it is presently unclear exactly when the family of Paola Elisabetta (*Betta*) L'Abbate became involved in fishing, it is known that several generations of fishermen in her family lived in Terrasini before emigrating to Gloucester in the early 1900s.

The family information of Paola is based on the genealogical research of Grace Parisi McArdle. Grace's mother, Mary Josephine Scola Parisi and Madeline Scola Ventimiglia were first cousins who lived in Gloucester. Madeline was the grandmother of Francis Joseph Ventimiglia, my husband. These Scola families are descendants of Sebastiano Scola and Maria Crocifissa (Josephine) Brancaleone Scola, one of the early Italian immigrant families to settle in Gloucester. Paola and her family are ancestors of Maria Crocifissa (Josephine) Brancaleone. With Grace's generous permission I used them as the characters in *The Women of Light: Betta's Story*, which takes place in the neighborhood where the Scola ancestors lived during the 1800s in Terrasini and at their church, *la Chiesa di Santa Rosalia* with its current *piazzetta*.

Votive Offerings

The miniature of Matteo's boat is known as a votive offering or ex-voto. Votive offerings show devotion or gratitude to God or a saint for interceding on behalf of a devotee, in thanks for a prayer answered, a miracle bestowed, or in anticipation of a miracle yet to come. Ex-votos can take many forms and perhaps the most common is the lighting of votive candles found in churches. In many coastal churches, boats or ships are also offered as ex-votos for the protection of a loved one at sea.

In Terrasini, the most obvious examples of ex-votos in today's churches are votive candles. The meaningful significance of various other forms, however, fit the story and offered a further glimpse into the devotion of the village.

The Statue of San Pietro

A statue of *San Pietro,* patron saint of fishermen, stands in a niche in today's church of *Maria Ss. Della Provvidenza,* known as the church of the fishermen, built later in Terrasini's history. However, the statue is portrayed in "*Betta's Story*" as being in *la Chiesa di Santa Rosalia* and holding fishing boat votive offerings.

Lucerne

Following the hand gestures Vincenza Randazzo used when she described the scene on the beach, I envisioned a vessel that could easily be held, cupped in a person's hand. A search of possibilities led me to the covered terracotta *lucerne,* the lamps that could have been used at the time to light homes.

The Bells of Santa Rosalia

It is true, though, that it would have been the bells of *la Chiesa di Santa Rosalia* that rang out that day. There are currently numerous churches in Terrasini, yet only *Santa Rosalia*, built in the late 17th century, had a bell tower in 1726. The mother church, *Maria SS. delle Grazie*, was constructed in 1713 on the site of a small chapel initially built in 1683. But her bell towers were added much later in 1908. The church of *Maria Ss. Della*

Provvidenza was built in 1923, also from a small chapel, and was established as its own parish in 1953. Other churches and small chapels grace the beautiful town of Terrasini, a community still steeped in its faith.

ACKNOWLEDGMENTS

How does a writer ever begin to fully thank those who helped bring a story idea to life? A few words on a page do not seem enough, so to all, please know my heartfelt thanks go much deeper than any sentiment written here. *Grazie. Mille Grazie a tutti.*

The dream that led to this novelette was invited by Vincenza Randazzo, a vibrant woman committed to preserving local Sicilian histories and linking people with their Sicilian families, ancestors, and heritage.

When the dream appeared, I was in it, living it. I felt the connection of family, so I turned to my husband's Terrasini ancestors for names, for the family who, in my dream, lived through that day in September 1726. The incredible family research of Grace Parisi McArdle, a native of Gloucester, provided a way to personalize this story and its meaning.

The encouragement to write this story and the belief that I could do it, most avidly, came from Wayne Soini. A history buff and author of more than 30 books, he is supportive of any fellow author who crosses his path, and with this author he also exercised great patience.

Writing can be a lonely journey, yet sharing with colleagues offers a supportive forum for constructive feedback which I was lucky enough to receive from my writers' group, particularly Danuta, George, Lise, Bill, Dan, Susan, and Wayne.

Researching the nuances of a life lived within the context of historical times is always a challenge. With this story, the help of Maria (Mia) Millefoglie was invaluable.

The final version of this story would not be as robust without the insight, comments, and suggestions from these readers: Grace Ventimiglia Simpson, Beth Simpson, Wayne Soini, Laura Jones Ventimiglia, Arwen Severance, Lynn Clarkson, and Diletta Ballati.

Of course, every author needs a production team. Terry Weber Mangos proved to be the perfect editor. She truly honored the story, respected my voice, and was steadfast in every step of the publication process. Camille Vicenti, a talented and gracious book designer, offered that same commitment to the book's development. Together their talents contributed to a quality publication.

Allie Nicastro, an illustrator whose ancestors emigrated from Terrasini to Gloucester, was a vivacious and creative collaborator.

Diletta Ballati and Alicia Ballati, from Northern Italy who are equally at home in Gloucester and Terrasini, cheerfully provided their translation services, encouragement, love for family history and our shared Italian heritage. Diletta, who served as a reader, but also as the translator of *Betta's Story*, is my partner in all my Italian projects, and Alicia was with me on that day in January 2020 when I heard the legend from Vincenza.

Finally, my family and husband, Frank Ventimiglia, have always believed in me and supported me in following my dreams.

Le Donne della Luce:
La Storia di Betta

È il 21 settembre 1740, il giorno della festa di San Matteo. Matteo è scomparso da dodici anni. Io e mia figlia Francesca stiamo preparando dei dolci per l'onomastico di Matteo, il giorno del suo Santo patrono di cui portava il nome.

Abbiamo sempre festeggiato questo giorno quando Matteo era ancora in vita. Una grande cena per il suo onomastico. A quei tempi, il mio Matteo era alto e magro ma robusto, con la pelle olivastra, i capelli neri e folti in alto sulla testa, e i baffi perfetti sotto il naso. Sedeva al posto d'onore a tavola, con tutta la famiglia Palazzolo stretta attorno come pesci nelle reti tirate su dalle barche nel nostro villaggio di pescatori. I nostri figli, Giovanni e Domenico, sedevano alla sua sinistra; io ero alla sua destra, vicino alla stufa, sempre pronta a portare in tavola il piatto successivo. Una giovane Francesca sedeva accanto a me, e spesso la tavola era adornata con un piccolo mazzetto di fiori di campo che raccoglieva per suo padre.

I suoni nell'aria erano sempre allegri, le forchette che tintinnavano al ritmo delle voci, interrotte solo dai bocconi di cibo. Si festeggiava con piatti piatti di pasta, pesce con le verdure di Vito, il venditore di quartiere, che vendeva sul carretto all'angolo, formaggi e frutta, e i fichi d'India che erano i nostri preferiti. Una tale abbondanza era riservata alle occasioni speciali nella nostra povera famiglia di pescatori.

All'altro capo della tavola c'erano Nonno Battista, il padre di Matteo, e Nonna Giovanna, sua madre, che aiutava a servire i piatti man mano che li portavo. Francesco, il fratello minore di Matteo, si assicurava che le brocche di vino e acqua fossero sempre piene. Ahh, avere acqua potabile era un vero piacere. Allora, come oggi, andavamo ogni giorno alla fontana pubblica in piazza, dove incontravamo i vicini, chiacchieravamo e riempivamo le nostre brocche, pesanti e traboccanti, da portare a casa. Concludevamo il pasto con una torta di marzapane, il dolce preferito di Matteo. Ma prima di lasciare la tavola, e prima che Giuseppa, la moglie di Francesco, iniziasse a sistemare, e che Anna, la loro giovane figlia, se ne andasse ridendo e scherzando con Francesca, ci passavamo un'ultima volta il vino per fare un brindisi al nostro Matteo.

Oh, come ricordo quei giorni. Oh, come Matteo riusciva a sciogliermi il cuore con un solo sguardo. Se solo fosse ancora con noi. Ah, Matteo.

Per onorarlo e ricordare la sua vita, continuiamo a celebrare il suo onomastico con dei dolci: Cassateddi di ricotta, Giuggiulena, e la sua amata torta di marzapane. Mi aiuta a sentirmi vicina a lui e a mantenere vivo il suo ricordo nella nostra famiglia. Oggi mentre io e Francesca cuciniamo, i miei nipoti — Rosa, Carlo e Alessandro — giocano ai nostri piedi.

«Mamma,» dice Francesca, «racconta ai bambini di quando hai salvato Nonno Matteo e il nostro villaggio.»

Rosa interviene, «Per favore, Nonna Betta! Amo questa storia!»

«Una storia, sì!» grida Carlo alzando le braccia.

Alessandro mi tira la gonna, «Storia. Storia.»

«Va bene. Venite qui,» dico loro. «D'accordo, d'accordo. Venite qui con me.»

Mi accomodo sulla sedia di legno nell'angolo vicino alla finestra. La sua vernice turchese screpolata e il cuscino fiorito ormai consumato mi ricordano il giorno del mio matrimonio. Era un regalo dei genitori di Matteo, per accogliermi nella loro famiglia. Ogni volta che mi siedo lì, sento l'abbraccio del loro amore e l'amore di Matteo. Le imposte della finestra sono aperte alle voci dei nostri vicini e alla luce intensa del giorno.

Rosa arriva saltellando e cantando, «È stata una bella giornata!» Carlo le gira intorno danzando. Tutti ridono, sapendo cosa sta per arrivare, mentre lei continua a cantare, «È stata una bella giornata!» Carlo si arrampica sulle mie ginocchia. Rosa si accoccola ai miei piedi tenendo Alessandro in braccio. Il sole illumina i loro volti impazienti. Un silenzio cala sulla stanza. Comincio, come sempre . . .

Era una bella giornata, era proprio una bella giornata! Poteva sembrare un giorno di giugno, d'inizio d'estate, ma non lo era. Nel nostro piccolo villaggio di pescatori, Terrasini, era domenica 1 settembre 1726. Dal balcone fuori dalla porta della nostra camera da letto, potevo vedere il porto. Guardavo le barche dei pescatori salpare verso il mare, oltre la Torre Mulinazzo, la torre di pietra che veglia contro gli avversari che si avvicinano dal mare lungo la nostra costa. Nella luce dell'alba, rosso-arancio, riflessa sull'oceano, riuscivo a distinguere la barca di legno di Matteo tra le altre, con il suo audace bordo blu dipinto sopra i vivaci colori dell'arancione, del bianco e dell'ocra gialla. Mentre remava, l'albero e la vela riposavano accanto a lui, lungo il lato di dritta. La sua routine mi era familiare. Fuori dal porto, montava l'albero e issava la vela.

Salutai con la mano. Sapevo che Matteo non poteva vedermi, oppure sì? In quel giorno, domenica, il nostro tempo sacro insieme ogni settimana, stava forse guardando con nostalgia verso casa, rammaricandosi di essere lontano dalla famiglia? Sarebbe stato con noi, se non fosse stato per la povertà del nostro villaggio e l'abbondanza di pesce nei nostri mari.

Sì, ricordo bene quella bellissima giornata, con la luce intensa del mattino che riempiva il cielo azzurro, senza una nuvola. La pace che si respirava. Eppure, iniziai ad agitare le braccia freneticamente, desiderando che mi vedesse. Una sensazione bruciante attraversò il mio corpo. Cos'era? Cos'era quell'urgenza di fargli vedere che ero lì, come se potesse essere l'ultima volta? Mi rimproverai, «Betta, smettila di essere così emotiva. Matteo starà bene.»

Le barche da pesca, la sua barca, ormai erano fuori dalla mia vista. Salutai un'ultima volta, con malinconia, senza voler lasciar andare. Quando rientrai in camera, un brivido mi attraversò il corpo. Nonostante il calore del primo mattino, rabbrividii.

Camminai in punta di piedi attraverso la cucina fino alla cameretta sul retro. Era troppo presto per svegliare i bambini, ma avevo bisogno di vederli. Aprii con delicatezza la porta che cigolava per dare un'occhiata a Francesca, che aveva otto anni. La sua bambola di pezza stretta tra le braccia, i capelli castani e ondulati sparsi delicatamente sul cuscino, e un sorriso sulle labbra, come se gli angeli le stessero raccontando una meravigliosa storia nel sonno. Scostai la tenda che la separava dai fratelli e guardai dentro. Dormivano profondamente. Domenico, undici anni da vero selvatico era tutto aggrovigliato nelle coperte. Giovanni, quindici anni, alto e forte come suo padre, normalmente sarebbe stato fuori a pescare con lui. Ma, mentre Matteo si alzava dal letto nel buio delle prime ore del mattino, mi sussurrò, «Betta, lascia dormire il ragazzo. Può restare a casa oggi e aiutare te.»

Tornai in cucina, grata per l'amore che Matteo aveva per la nostra famiglia. Il sole cominciava a mostrarsi in tutta la sua bellezza, un sentiero luminoso verso il cielo che filtrava attraverso le fessure delle porte di legno. Le spalancai. La luce intensa entrò, sollevando il mio spirito e riempiendo ogni angolo della stanza con la sua energia. La luce danzante portava la mia preghiera per la sicurezza di Matteo in giro per la stanza, fuori dalla porta e su, fino al nostro Padre Celeste. La protezione calda di quella giornata di sole mi avvolse. Cominciai a cantare piano e a danzare intorno al tavolo. Stavo preparando una piccola delizia per la colazione: pane caldo appena sfornato, cosparso d'olio d'oliva aromatizzato al rosmarino e con altre erbe che avevo raccolto dalla terra secca e screpolata più in alto, verso i confini del paese. È proprio una bella giornata!

Un fruscio alle mie spalle annunciò il risveglio dei bambini. Arrivarono uno dopo l'altro in cucina, sbadigliando, strofinandosi gli occhi, stiracchiando le braccia verso il soffitto. Ridendo del mio buonumore, si unirono alla mia danza. Gira e rigira, danzavamo tutti insieme. Domenico tirò i capelli a Francesca. Le sue urla divertite lo deliziarono. Lei cercò di afferrare i suoi riccioli neri rimbalzanti, ma mancò il bersaglio. Ridacchiando e stuzzicandosi a vicenda, si tuffarono infine sulle sedie attorno al tavolo.

La bellezza di quella giornata arrivava fino a noi, alla nostra famiglia. Domenico e Francesca giocavano allegramente, senza i soliti litigi per questo o per quello, senza spinte o sgomitate che spesso finivano con uno dei due che urtava il tavolo, facendolo traballare quasi fino a farlo cadere, senza il latte del mattino che gocciolava giù, giù, giù fino al pavimento, senza cibo che volava per aria e usciva dalle porte del balcone, finendo per nutrire il cane pigro che dorme tutto il giorno al sole della Piazza Duomo.

Ci sedemmo intorno al tavolo, ridendo e chiacchierando, felici di essere insieme ma con un grande vuoto per l'assenza di Matteo. Parlare di lui ci faceva sentire come se fosse lì con noi, così cominciammo a fare progetti per il suo ritorno a casa. Improvvisamente, le campane della Chiesa di Santa Rosalia iniziarono a suonare, annunciando l'inizio della giornata. «Via, via!» dissi. «Presto, sistemate tutto e preparatevi per la Messa. Andiamo!»

Scendendo le scale di casa nostra, incontrammo Giuseppa e Anna nel corridoio. Anche Francesco era uscito per andare a pesca. Vivevamo tutti insieme nella casa di Nonno Battista e Nonna Giovanna. Francesco e la sua famiglia abitavano con loro al piano terra, mentre noi stavamo nelle stanze al piano di sopra.

«Nonna Giovanna e Nonno Battista non sono ancora pronti,» disse Giuseppa. «Dobbiamo aspettare.»

Giuseppa era mia amica. Condividevamo un legame di sorellanza, vivendo nella stessa casa, prendendoci cura delle famiglie l'una dell'altra e dei genitori dei nostri mariti. Giuseppa era la giovane prudente della casa e cercava in me forza e guida. Per me, Giuseppa era una confidente fidata. Potevo sempre condividere con lei idee, pensieri o opinioni, e sapevo di poter contare sulla sua sincerità e sul suo sostegno ogni volta che ne avevo bisogno.

Rimanemmo appena fuori dalla porta di casa ad aspettare Nonno Battista e Nonna Giovanna, mentre salutavamo e chiamavamo i nostri vicini che passavano sulla via per andare a Messa, «Buon giorno! Buon giorno! Buona domenica!»

Io e Giuseppa prendemmo ciascuna un braccio di Nonna e Nonno. Camminammo lentamente su per la collina del nostro villaggio di montagna. Sentivamo il caldo di quella splendida giornata mentre affrontavamo la ripida salita. La Chiesa di Santa Rosalia, all'inizio del nostro quartiere, fece risuonare di nuovo le sue campane. La Messa stava per cominciare. I bambini corsero avanti. Ancora una volta Domenico iniziò a stuzzicare Francesca, questa volta saltellandole intorno e facendo smorfie buffe. Giovanni intervenne come avrebbe fatto suo padre, e lo sentii dire, «Domenico, basta! Lascia stare Francesca. Sta' attento.» Sorrisi, felice di vedere la nostra famiglia unita.

Raggiungemmo i gradini della Chiesa di Santa Rosalia, con i suoi alti portoni di legno intagliato. Proprio mentre stavo entrando, sentii un sussurro all'orecchio, «Betta, oh Betta.» Mi voltai verso la voce e vidi solo il lontano oceano azzurro chiaro, glorioso sotto il cielo limpido e il sole splendente. La pelle mi si accapponò e un brivido mi salì lungo la schiena. Cosa stava succedendo? Nel confondersi di quel momento, vidi Matteo. Stava bene. Forte e concentrato sul suo lavoro, con i muscoli in tensione, stava tirando su una rete piena di pesci dal lato della sua barca. Scossi la testa per scacciare quella visione.

All'interno della Chiesa le pareti di pietra bianca mantenevano l'aria fresca e piacevole, offrendo sollievo dal caldo opprimente dell'esterno. Le voci dei nostri vicini ci accolsero cantando. La statua della Madonna del Rosario con il bambino in grembo nella nicchia sopra l'altare, ci dava il benvenuto. Le immagini dei santi su tela vegliavano su di noi. Una statua di San Pietro, il santo patrono dei pescatori, si ergeva imponente nella sua nicchia. Guardai la barchetta in miniatura di Matteo, appesa lì sotto, insieme a quelle di altre famiglie di pescatori. Pregai per la sua sicurezza in mare, come faccio sempre. Quando ci siamo sposati, Matteo intagliò quella barchetta, la dipinse come la sua vera imbarcazione e me la regalò, perché potessi sentirlo vicino quando era via a pescare. La portai qui nella nostra chiesa e la appesi come offerta. Ho offerto quella piccola barca in segno di gratitudine a San Pietro e a Dio per la costante protezione di Matteo. Pensandolo, immaginandolo proprio come l'avevo visto poco prima — con la rete piena di pesci — un sorriso mi sfiorò le labbra e un'ondata d'affetto mi riempì il cuore.

Don Paolo, immerso nella sua devozione, entrò dalla sacrestia, la sua voce si unì alla nostra in un'esplosione di giubilo. La Messa ebbe inizio. Mi sedetti sulla nostra panca, rilassata, sapendo di essere benedetta. Sapevo che la fede era l'anima del paese, e le nostre famiglie il cuore. Non avevamo bisogno di alcun monito sulla furia che poteva abbattersi su di noi, né sulla punizione divina in caso di disobbedienza al Signore, perché tutto ciò che facevamo allora — e continuiamo a fare oggi — lo facevamo e lo facciamo volentieri, al servizio di Dio e del prossimo. Vegliavamo gli uni sugli altri e sui bambini del nostro paese. Quando il pesce scarseggiava, sfamavamo le famiglie altrui; quando c'erano compleanni, ci riunivamo; quando un bambino, una moglie o un marito si ammalava, ce ne prendevamo cura; quando la fortuna bussava alla porta di una famiglia, gioivamo tutti insieme. E perché no? Sui faraglioni, quelle formazioni rocciose che ornano la riva, sul mare, sulle grotte e sulle montagne che circondano il nostro villaggio, sapevamo che il Signore Dio Onnipotente, ci stava accanto, abbracciandoci con la sua protezione. Insieme celebravamo le nostre fortune. Insieme, aiutandoci a vicenda, affrontavamo la povertà e le difficoltà. Quel giorno eravamo sereni nella nostra felicità. Protetti dal mondo esterno, al sicuro nel nostro piccolo paese incastonato nella conca ai piedi delle montagne, le stesse montagne che impedivano al mondo di irrompere nella nostra vita.

La Messa terminò. Liberati nel caldo torrido del giorno inoltrato lasciammo Santa Rosalia. Attirati dalla spiaggia e dalle sue acque fresche e tranquille, riscendemmo la collina più in fretta di quanto l'avessimo salita, la terra sembrava tirarci i piedi giù, giù, giù. Arrivammo sulla porta di casa, a pochi passi dalla scogliera che si affaccia sul mare. Uno spettacolo splendido ci accolse: il mare azzurro e scintillante in lontananza, che faceva capolino oltre le rocce imponenti, coperte di ciuffi d'erba selvatica e fiori. Nella mia mente vidi Matteo. Era là fuori, da qualche parte, a pescare per noi. Il suo amore tornava indietro fino a me. Un lungo respiro profondo gonfiò il mio petto e uscì dalla mia bocca. Ahhh, un momento bellissimo in una giornata meravigliosa.

La Nonna e il Nonno entrarono in casa per riposarsi. Giuseppa, i bambini ed io continuammo a camminare lungo il ripido sentiero tortuoso che ci conduceva giù, tra le rocce frastagliate, fino alla sabbia fine e marrone della nostra spiaggia. Per fortuna il caldo Scirocco non soffiava su di noi. Era una giornata perfetta, mentre l'estate volgeva al termine. L'acqua cristallina blu scuro e turchese, scivolava verso la spiaggia sopra il fondale sabbioso increspato e si avvolgeva attorno ai faraglioni. I raggi di sole filtravano da un cielo senza nuvole e scintille di luce danzavano sulla superficie dell'acqua. Francesca e Anna corsero verso il bagnasciuga, ballando e schizzando ovunque. I ragazzi si tuffarono in acqua, e subito i vestiti si appiccicarono alla pelle, nuotavano e si immergevano come pesci giganti. I presagi del mattino erano ormai dimenticati, cancellati dalla bellezza e dalla pace di quella giornata; mi sedetti con Giuseppa sulla sabbia.

Giuseppa, con una nota di preoccupazione nella voce, disse, «Mi preoccupo sempre di più per Nonna Giovanna e Nonno Battista. Si stancano facilmente e sembrano così fragili.»

«L'ho notato anch'io,» risposi, «e deve essere difficile vivere nelle stesse stanze con loro e prendersene cura quando hanno bisogno d'aiuto, senza però farli sentire dipendenti da te, senza farli sentire vecchi e decrepiti.»

«Lo è,» disse Giuseppa, «so che tu sei al piano di sopra per aiutare, ma mi dispiace tanto per loro. Sono sempre stati così pieni di vita.»

«Lo so. E se iniziassimo a fare tutte le riunioni di famiglia a casa tua, così non dovrebbero salire le scale fino da noi?»

«Sarebbe meraviglioso. Una grande idea. Grazie.»

«E io farò di più per aiutarti giù, al piano di sotto.»

La nostra conversazione divenne più leggera. Lasciammo che il calore del sole ci accarezzasse e osservammo i nostri bambini giocare felici. Sapevamo, nel profondo del cuore, che la nostra ricchezza nasceva dall'amore delle nostre famiglie e dalla sicurezza del nostro bellissimo, piccolo paese.

Carlo mi salta in grembo, battendo le mani. «Nonna, dopo questa storia possiamo andare al mare?»

«Mmm, sembra divertente.»

«Shh,» dice Rosa, «voglio sentire la storia di Nonna Betta e ora Alessandro è tutto agitato.»

«Ma io voglio andare al mare. Mi piace quando andiamo al mare. Nonna, posso mostrarti come so nuotare. Per favore?»

«Ricordi che stiamo preparando una festa per l'onomastico del Nonno Matteo?»

«Ma dopo che avrò nuotato possiamo scavare nella sabbia e tu puoi aiutarmi a costruire un fortino. Scommetto che anche Alessandro vuole costruire un fortino. Per favore? Per favore?»

«Va bene, andremo al mare dopo aver festeggiato il Nonno Matteo. Ora, torniamo alla storia.»

Il pavimento si è mosso. Si è mosso il pavimento? Con le spalle alla porta aperta della cucina, ero china sul tavolo al centro della stanza a stendere la pasta per la cena a base di pasta con le sarde. Avevamo deciso di sorprendere Matteo con un banchetto al suo ritorno a casa per celebrare quel giorno glorioso e fargli sapere quanto ci era mancato. Le sardine, le preferite di

Matteo, erano quasi sempre nella sua rete. Ero sicura che quella sera avremmo potuto contare su di loro per la nostra cena. Il dolce aroma di anice del finocchio selvatico che avevo tagliato in precedenza riempiva l'aria. Più tardi l'avrei mescolato con le sardine e per poi cuocerli nell'olio d'oliva.

Mi scostai le ciocche di capelli dalla fronte e sognai Matteo. All'improvviso fui accecata da un'oscurità soffocante che si era insinuata dietro di me attraverso le porte aperte. Il mio cuore si fermò. Poi riprese a battere sempre più velocemente. Che cosa stava succedendo?

Il pavimento è tremato di nuovo. Un leggero tremore, appena percettibile, ma questa volta ne sono sicura. Sentii la scopa nell'angolo battere sul muro a ritmo delle stoviglie che sicuramente stavano danzando mentre sbattevano l'una contro l'altra sui loro scaffali. Rimasi in piedi, all'erta. Lontano, molto lontano, sentii un boato sordo.

Mi girai leggermente, appoggiandomi al tavolo, e affrontai il buio. Sentii delle urla provenire dall'esterno. Non era mai successo nulla di simile. Cosa stava succedendo al nostro paese?

Oh Mio Dio! I bambini. Dove erano i bambini? Gridavo i loro nomi Francesca! Domenico! Giovanni! Nessuna risposta. Il mattarello mi cadde dalle mani con un colpo secco. La farina volò in aria, colpendomi in faccia e intorno a me. Giovanni stava andando in piazzetta a prendere l'acqua potabile alla fontana pubblica per la cena. Forse aveva portato con sé Domenico e Francesca. Urlai chiamando Giuseppa. Nessuna risposta. Dov'era? Dov'era Anna? Dov'erano Nonno Battista e Nonna Giovanna? Cercando di orientarmi, inciampai lungo la rampa di scale senza riuscire a vedere dove stavo andando. Urlai di nuovo i loro nomi per tutto il tragitto. Francesca! Domenico! Giovanni! Giuseppa! Anna! Nonno! Nonna!

La gente si riversò fuori dalle case. Grida. Grida. Caos. Cercai di correre tra la folla, con la gonna lunga raccolta nella mano destra e la mano sinistra come guida. Era buio pesto. Il nostro pomeriggio soleggiato era scomparso, inghiottito da quella che sembrava essere una gigantesca nuvola nera e furiosa. Riuscivo a vedere dove stavo andando solo quando ero lì, un passo alla volta. I miei piedi scivolavano sui ciottoli della terra. Le campane della Chiesa di Santa Rosalia rintoccarono all'impazzata, lanciando un allarme così veloce e forte che l'aspro scoppio metallico rimbombò nelle mie orecchie. Mi diressi verso la nostra chiesa e la Piazzetta Santa Rosalia, sperando che i miei figli fossero lì.

Un piede davanti all'altro mi costrinsi a salire la collina. Ansimavo mentre correvo, l'aria entrava di corsa ferendo i polmoni e bruciandoli a ogni respiro. Il cuore mi batteva forte. Mi strinsi il petto per alleviare il dolore.

Dov'erano i miei figli? Dov'era la nostra famiglia? Cosa stava succedendo al nostro paese? L'oscurità minacciosa era più terrificante di qualsiasi cosa avessi mai immaginato. La gigantesca nuvola nera si abbassò intorno a noi e strinse la sua morsa sull'intera città. E perché il terreno continuava a muoversi, anche se solo leggermente? Per favore Cara Santa Rosalia, proteggi i miei figli! Proteggi i nostri figli! Proteggi il nostro villaggio! Cara Maria Santissima delle Grazie, prega per noi, prega per noi.

Ho sentito la voce familiare di Giuseppa che gridava alla ricerca di Anna. «Giuseppa,» gridai.

«Betta,» urlò Giuseppa, «hai visto Anna?»

«No. Dove sono Nonna Giovanna e Nonno Battista?»

«Stanno bene, sono in casa ma hanno paura. Ho detto loro di stare lì, di stare vicini e di non muoversi.»

I vicini si urlavano l'un l'altro. Ho sentito gli amici chiamare il mio nome. «Betta, cosa facciamo?», gridò Antonina. «Betta, ho paura per il mio Salvatore,» chiamò Vincenza, «puoi aiutarmi a trovarlo?» «Betta,» gridò Maria, «non so dove sia andato a giocare il mio piccolo Nunzio.»

Il dolore ai polmoni e al cuore non bastarono per fermare la mia corsa contro il tempo per ritrovare i miei figli, erano sufficienti pochi secondi per riprendere fiato. Mi chinai con le mani sulle ginocchia per far riposare il mio corpo. Ma solo una frazione di secondo. La folla di madri in cerca dei loro figli mi spingeva ad andare avanti. Circondate da una fitta nebbia di paura, corremmo insieme nella nostra frenetica ricerca.

Urlavo, o cercavo di urlare, ma le parole uscivano ormai in un sussurro, «Francesca, Domenico, Giovanni, dove siete?»

Mi incamminai a passi più lunghi verso la collina, respirando più pesantemente e scivolando mentre andavo avanti. Le mie anche, affaticate dai lunghi passi che mi portavano su, su, su, si univano al dolore nel petto. La salita alla Chiesa di Santa Rosalia e alla sua piazzetta sembrava più ripida di quanto ricordassi. Avrei voluto fermarmi di nuovo, ma non potevo. Ero quasi arrivata e non ero sola. Il nugolo di madri mi portava con sé. Nell'oscurità ci urtavamo l'una con l'altra, inciampando, ma continuavamo la nostra ricerca. Le nostre voci lottavano per farsi sentire l'una sull'altra e sulle campane della chiesa mentre gridavamo alla ricerca dei nostri figli.

Il ronzio nelle mie orecchie si scontrava con le urla nella mia testa, «Figli miei, figli miei dove siete?» Cercai di gridare ancora, «Francesca, Domenico,

Giovanni,» ma i loro nomi mi rimasero impressi nella secchezza della bocca, asciugati dall'aria che entrava a fiotti nei miei polmoni in fiamme. «Per favore, per favore Caro Gesù, ti prego, ti prego caro Gesù, proteggi i miei figli. Cara Maria Santissima delle Grazie, prega per noi, prega per noi.» Poteva Dio sentire le mie preghiere al di sopra del martellare del mio cuore e del ronzio nelle orecchie? Era possibile che le mie preghiere silenziose raggiungessero il mondo celeste?

Raggiunsi la piazzetta. Udii un rombo di voci e riconobbi quella di Giovanni. La mia voce si levò contro il dolore nel mio corpo, contro le campane della chiesa, contro le altre voci, e urlai sempre più forte, «Giovanni! Giovanni!» urlavo ancora e ancora. Finalmente mi ha sentito e ha seguito la mia voce finché non ho sentito il suo abbraccio. Grazie Santa Rosalia. Grazie mille Caro Gesù. Grazie Cara Maria. Era al sicuro e con lui c'era Domenico che si aggrappava alla mia vita. Spinti dalle altre madri che correvano, ci siamo abbracciati forte, grati di esserci ritrovate. Ma dov'era Francesca? Povera bambina spaventata, dove sei?

Stringendoci per non separarci, siamo tornati verso casa, spingendoci delicatamente attraverso la calca di madri in preda al panico. Continuavamo a urlare, «Francesca! Francesca! Francesca!»

Abbiamo controllato tutti i suoi nascondigli preferiti. Abbiamo chiesto alle famiglie dei suoi amici, «Hai visto la nostra Francesca? Francesca Palazzolo?» Niente. Niente. Oh no! La spiaggia e il porto. Non ci va mai da sola, ma se si fosse persa? Confusa? Oh Mio Dio, Oh Santa Madre Maria, potrebbe essere finita in acqua?

Abbiamo raggiunto la nostra casa. Nonna Giovanna e Nonno Battista erano in piedi bloccati sulla soglia. «Giovanni,» ho supplicato, «corri di sopra e cerca Francesca in casa. Domenico e io resteremo qui e ci prenderemo cura dei Nonni per assicurarci che stiano bene.»

L'ho sentito salire le scale nel nulla torbido, gridando, «Francesca! Francesca! Francesca, sei qui?» Poi più niente.

Avvolto dall'oscurità e dal rumore della folla, il mio cuore batteva come se dovesse scoppiare da un momento all'altro. Un ronzio mi martellava ancora nelle orecchie. Le grida dei bambini spaventati provenivano dalle finestre aperte. Gonne e piedi si trascinavano spinti dalle madri in preda al panico che gridavano alla ricerca dei loro figli – Sara, Caterina, Ninfa – dove sei? Ho abbracciato Nonna Giovanna e ho accarezzato la spalla del Nonno Battista. Tremavano entrambi. Allora ho fatto cambio. Ho abbracciato il Nonno e stretto la mano alla Nonna. Per tutto il tempo pregavo in silenzio. «Per favore, per favore Dio, fa che Francesca sia al sicuro. Santa Madre Maria prega per Francesca, prega per noi.»

Poi la sentii. Una vocina flebile che si avvicinava sempre di più. «Mamma. Mamma.»

Giovanni l'aveva trovata! Aveva trovato anche Anna. Esauste dopo un pomeriggio trascorso a giocare con i cugini, si erano addormentate abbracciate insieme nel letto di Anna. Con una bambina impaurita per braccio, Giovanni emerse. Proprio in quel momento arrivò anche Giuseppa, correndo dalla spiaggia. Era andata a cercare Anna lì.

Di nuovo insieme, ci stringemmo nell'ingresso. Superando lentamente lo shock, cominciando a sperare che sarebbe andato tutto bene, ci rilassammo abbastanza da abbracciarci, baciarci e consolarci a vicenda, ancora e ancora. Iniziammo a riflettere e chiederci ad alta voce: cos'è successo? La grande nuvola nera ci copriva ancora, ma Ci eravamo ritrovati, ed eravamo di nuovo tutti insieme. Il quartiere cominciava a calmarsi mentre le famiglie si riunivano. Eravamo al sicuro. Sfiancati, rientrammo in casa.

«Giovanni,» dissi, «dobbiamo portare un po' di luce qui dentro. Accendiamo le candele che teniamo da parte per i momenti speciali.»

«Ma Mamma,» rispose lui, «sono troppo costose. Costano troppo, e ne abbiamo solo poche. Perché non usiamo le lucerne, le nostre lampade a olio?»

«No, Giovanni. Tuo fratello e tua sorella devono sapere che andrà tutto bene. Le candele glielo faranno capire.» E dentro di me dissi, «Grazie, Dio Mio, grazie Santa Rosalia, grazie Maria Santissima delle Grazie, per la salvezza della mia famiglia.»

Ancora senza sapere cosa fosse successo al nostro piccolo paese, controllai velocemente la casa. Con solo il bagliore della candela dei bambini, mentre erano tutti stretti attorno al tavolo della cucina — la stanza dove passavamo le nostre giornate — mi mossi a tentoni. Giù al piano di sotto sapevo che Giuseppa stava facendo lo stesso. Ci gridammo l'un l'altra, «Va tutto bene.»

Feci un lungo respiro per calmarmi, mi appoggiai allo stipite della porta della cucina, le braccia incrociate a stringermi. Avevo paura di uscire sul balcone. Guardai fuori, nel nero abisso della nuvola che ancora soffocava il nostro villaggio. Il silenzio mi ruggì contro. Gli uccelli non cinguettavano. Le strade erano prive di suoni. I cespugli e il sottobosco sulle scogliere non frusciavano. Respiri brevi e affannosi iniziarono a salirmi in gola. Ansimando, il cuore mi batteva forte. Mi strinsi il petto per non soffocare, per cercare di riportare il respiro alla calma di pochi secondi prima, ma la paura si faceva strada.

Matteo! Cosa stava succedendo a lui là fuori, in mezzo al mare? Il nero si estendeva a perdita d'occhio. Offuscava la vista del cielo e della terra. I piccoli bagliori delle candele accese nelle case, che avrebbero potuto guidarlo verso il villaggio, erano nascosti dalla furia della nuvola nera. Senza quei punti luce a riva, senza la luce morente del giorno, come avrebbe fatto lui — come avrebbero fatto tutti i pescatori — a ritrovare la strada di casa? Come avrebbero trovato il porto ed evitato di schiantarsi contro gli scogli, dove si trovano la Torre Mulinazzo o i faraglioni lungo la costa? Avrebbero dovuto essere già di ritorno!

Gridai ai bambini, «State qui!» Li superai di corsa e scesi giù per le scale. Avevo un'idea. Caro Gesù, Cara Santa Rosalia, Cara Santa Madre Maria, vi prego, fate che funzioni. Bussando con forza alla porta di Nonno e Nonna urlai, «Aprite, aprite, dobbiamo aiutare i nostri uomini!» Giuseppa spalancò la porta, «Madonna mia!» esclamò.

Le esposi il mio piano e insieme lo riportammo alle donne del villaggio. Corremmo in strada gridando, chiamando le nostre vicine di casa. «Maria! Grazia! Giulia! Vincenza! Serafina! Antonina! Tutte le donne, venite subito!» Su e giù per la strada urlavamo, la voce sempre più forte, rivolte prima ad un lato della via e poi all'altro. Avanti e indietro, su e giù. Le donne uscirono in massa e si strinsero intorno a noi. Stretta dalla paura, il cuore che batteva all'impazzata, gridai, «Dobbiamo aiutare i pescatori! Ascoltate . . . »

«Betta,» disse Lucrezia, «non so. Ho paura, potrebbe essere pericoloso.»

Giuseppa intervenne, «È un'idea geniale. E pensate ai nostri uomini là fuori in mare. Per loro è ancora più pericoloso. Betta, io sono con te. Chi altro ci sta?»

Mormorii sommessi si sollevarono tra le donne. Aspettavo impaziente, le braccia incrociate, il piede che batteva nervoso. Il tempo passava e temevo che potessimo già essere in ritardo. Finalmente sentii delle voci gridare, «Sì! Sì! Vi aiutiamo. Lo faremo.»

La voce si diffuse di quartiere in quartiere, fino alla nostra Chiesa di Santa Rosalia e oltre, il piano per aiutare i nostri uomini a ritrovare la strada di casa.

«Nonna, ho paura!» Carlo gridò.

«Faceva paura. Ero terrorizzata. Ma sapevo che dovevo essere forte per Francesca, tua madre, che allora era solo una bambina, per i tuoi zii Domenico e Giovanni, per il Nonno Matteo, e per tutto il nostro villaggio.»

«Questa parte della storia non mi piace,» si lamentò Carlo.

«Faceva paura, ma credevo anche che il nostro Dio, Maria Santissima delle Grazie e Santa Rosalia si sarebbero presi cura di noi.»

Rosa allungò la mano e prese quella di Carlo, mentre Alessandro si accoccolava in grembo a lei.

«Carlo, shhh, questa è la parte più bella della storia. Ascolta.»

«Nonna, cosa è successo?» sussurrò Carlo.

Nel buio, le donne del nostro villaggio si divisero in due gruppi. Giuseppa ed io avremmo guidato un gruppo verso la spiaggia. Maria e Grazia avrebbero condotto l'altro verso la scogliera, circa trenta metri sopra di noi. Ero preoccupata per loro. Avevano il percorso più pericoloso da affrontare. Solo arrivare al bordo della scogliera sarebbe stata una camminata difficile, tra rocce, fessure, piante, sassolini e terra. Una volta lì, avrebbero affrontato lo stesso terreno irregolare, più il pericolo di avvicinarsi troppo al bordo e allo strapiombo. Tutto questo sarebbe già pericoloso alla luce del giorno, ora diventava mortale nell'oscurità che ci teneva prigioniere del terrore. Ma Maria e Grazia insistettero, sapendo che era ciò di cui i nostri uomini avevano bisogno. Ci abbracciammo, lasciando parlare i nostri cuori. Non servivano parole. Decise, ci incamminammo ognuna per la propria strada, guidate appena da deboli bagliori provenienti da alcune delle nostre lucerne.

Giuseppa ed io ci facemmo lentamente strada verso la spiaggia, scendendo il ripido sentiero serpeggiante, levigato dagli anni. Nel buio, tutte facevamo piccoli passi, cercando il cammino con i piedi, i bambini stretti alle mani delle madri, delle sorelle o fratelli maggiori, o dei Nonni più che erano con noi, determinati ad aiutare. Era proprio la stessa spiaggia dove, quella mattina, Giuseppa ed io avevamo trascorso momenti sereni con i nostri bambini. Ricordavo le bambine che giocavano vicino alla riva e i ragazzi che nuotavano e si tuffavano come pesci giganti. Ricordavo la sensazione di sicurezza, quel sentirsi protetti dall'amore delle nostre famiglie, raccolti nel nostro piccolo villaggio ai piedi delle montagne, al riparo dal mondo. Non avrei mai pensato che saremmo tornati lì, in mezzo ad un'oscurità spaventosa e misteriosa. Non avrei mai pensato che la pace del nostro villaggio potesse essere infranta, e il nostro mondo capovolto. Non avrei mai pensato che saremmo stati noi a dover salvare i pescatori di Terrasini. Il cuore mi saltò un battito, poi un altro, e un altro ancora. Il respiro si fece affannoso. Tentai di controllarlo mentre il mio corpo tremava. Le mani mi tremavano. La mente correva. E se il piano non avesse funzionato?

Poi ricordai la Messa di quella mattina e quella sensazione di sicurezza che mi aveva scaldato l'anima mentre sedevo sulla panca della Chiesa cantando le nostre preghiere. Ricordai da dove veniva quella sensazione: dal sapere che insieme, famiglie e vicini, affrontiamo le sfide e le gioie come un'unica comunità. Che insieme ci aiutiamo, e restiamo forti nella fede, perché sappiamo che il Signore Dio Onnipotente ci abbraccia nella Sua protezione. Il respiro si fece più calmo, le mani si fermarono, la mente si concentrò. Mi raddrizzai, le spalle dritte, il petto gonfio di fiducia, feci un passo in avanti rispetto alla folla e gridai, ripetendo il piano per riportare a casa i nostri uomini.

Sapevo che, forti della fede in Dio e nei Santi, eravamo in grado di affrontare quel compito.

Vestite di nero, ci confondevamo con il buio fitto della nube soffocante che ci teneva strette nella sua morsa. Le onde dell'oceano si infrangevano sulla riva. Non potevamo vederle, ma potevamo sentire le acque in tempesta. Le onde ruggivano come se spingessero da oltre la Torre Mulinazzo, vorticando e girando, arrivando veloci e schiantandosi furiosamente sulla costa. Qualcosa stava accadendo sott'acqua. Qualcosa che non potevamo vedere, ma di cui percepivamo la violenza. Eppure l'aria salmastra era immobile e fresca, il calore del giorno raffreddato dall'oscurità che ci circondava. Non eri mai successo niente di simile: le acque in tempesta mentre l'aria restava quieta. In quell'atmosfera inquietante, il sangue mi si gelò nelle vene e un senso di angoscia mi travolse.

La sabbia bagnata e appiccicosa, fredda senza il sole a scaldarla, si attaccava agli orli dei nostri abiti. Strisciando sulla sabbia umida, i vestiti si inzuppavano, così come le suole delle scarpe, l'umidità che lentamente ci saliva ai piedi.

Le campane di Santa Rosalia risuonavano, segnalando la posizione del nostro villaggio. I pescatori avrebbero sicuramente riconosciuto il suono delle due campane, una grande e una piccola, appese una accanto all'altra nella torre che sorge salda sul bordo del tetto della chiesa. Tirate con forza dalle loro lunghe corde, i campanari mandavano il loro messaggio in sequenze di suoni acuti e gravi verso il mare, per guidare gli uomini verso la riva della loro amata Terrasini.

Armate delle nostre lucerne, lampade di terracotta coperte, di ogni dimensione, che avevamo portato da casa insieme all'olio d'oliva per alimentarle e a strisce di stoffa da usare come stoppini, eravamo determinate a riportare i nostri uomini a casa. Sapevamo che, preparando le lucerne in modo diverso rispetto a come facevamo per illuminare le nostre case, avremmo potuto creare una fiamma più grande e duratura. Sapevamo anche che le fiamme si sarebbero riflesse sui nostri abiti scuri, rendendo la luce dei fuochi più visibile attraverso la nube nera.

Usando le poche lucerne già accese ci mettemmo in gruppo e in silenzio ci preparammo. In ginocchio sulla sabbia umida, chine sulle lucerne, le mani si muovevano rapide, stabili, concentrate sull'importanza del nostro compito, mentre mandavamo le nostre preghiere al cielo. Cara Maria Santissima delle Grazie, prega per i nostri uomini, prega per noi. Per ogni lucerna, invece di tirare lo stoppino attraverso il foro del coperchio, toglievamo i coperchi e li lasciavamo da parte. Usavamo lunghe strisce di stoffa come stoppini, le arrotolavamo e le accumulavamo sul fondo della lucerna finché non fuoriuscivano dal bordo, poi le riempivamo con l'olio.

Quando fummo pronti, tutti si disposero in fila, fianco a fianco, spalla contro spalla, con i più piccoli seduti o distesi ai piedi delle madri o dei Nonni. Nelle mani aperte, con i palmi uniti a coppa, ognuno teneva la propria lucerna. Giulia ad un'estremità, Angelina all'altra, Giuseppa ed io al centro, con Margherita,

Vincenza, Serafina e Antonina — le loro lucerne erano già accese a ci guidavano nel nostro compito — camminavamo lungo la fila iniziando ad accendere le lucerne. Quelle che ancora dovevano essere accese. Speravo che Maria e Grazia stessero facendo lo stesso, sulla scogliera sopra di noi. Per favore Santa Rosalia. Per favore Madre Maria, fate che siano arrivate sane e salve alla scogliera.

Con gli acciarini avvolti intorno alle dita e alle nocche, li colpivamo con le pietre focaie. Le scintille calde cadevano sugli stoppini. Appena le scintille toccavano la stoffa, si soffiava con costanza per accendere la propria lucerna, si soffiava più e più volte, finché la fiamma non prendeva vita. Accendemmo le nostre, ci unimmo alla fila, ed eravamo pronte.

Nel silenzio della notte, ma con il frastuono furioso delle onde che si infrangevano e si agitavano, creammo una fiamma ardente e continua lungo tutta la curva della spiaggia. In alto sulla scogliera ardeva un'altra fiamma continua come la nostra. Oh Dio mio, grazie. Grazie Santa Rosalia. Grazie Madre Maria. Le fiamme si levavano verso il cielo illuminando le coste della nostra Terrasini. Diventammo noi stessi un mare di luce, per guidare i nostri uomini a casa, il punto di riferimento di cui avevano bisogno per ritrovare la via del ritorno, sani e salvi, verso il porto.

Trattenevamo tutti il respiro, silenziosi nella preghiera. Per favore, fa' che funzioni. Grazie, caro Gesù, grazie di riuscire a portare la nostra luce fino al mare, di farla brillare abbastanza da essere vista. Cara Santa Rosalia, Cara Madre Maria, per favore, riporta a casa i nostri uomini sani e salvi. Cara Maria Santissima delle Grazie, prega per i nostri uomini, prega per noi, prega per il nostro paese.

Le campane di Santa Rosalia continuavano a risuonare. Forti e costanti nel loro messaggio. Spingevano il loro suono oltre le acque turbolente.

Aspettavamo e aspettavamo. Ascoltavamo. Silenziose. Vigilanti. Le braccia tese, le fiamme delle nostre lucerne crescevano, il calore dei fuochi ci scaldava il viso. Mandavamo le nostre preghiere verso l'alto e verso il mare, per i nostri mariti, padri, fratelli, figli, zii, affinché tornassero sani e salvi. Fiduciose nelle capacità dei nostri uomini, aspettavamo pazienti. Fiduciose nel nostro Dio, pregavamo. Trattenevamo le paure, sapendo — sperando — che presto le nostre famiglie e il nostro paese si sarebbe riunito.

Aspettammo, con i nostri fuochi che brillavano intensamente contro i vestiti neri nei tempi più oscura. E aspettammo ancora. Le nostre preghiere silenziose trovarono una voce armoniosa. Prima in un sussurro, poi sempre più forte, le nostre voci si sollevarono insieme verso il cielo. Cara Maria Santissima delle Grazie, prega per i nostri uomini, prega per noi, prega per il nostro paese. Cara Maria Santissima delle Grazie, prega per i nostri uomini, prega per noi, prega per il nostro paese. Cara Maria Santissima delle Grazie, prega per i nostri uomini, prega per noi, prega per il nostro paese. Le campane della Chiesa suonavano senza sosta.

Poi lo sentimmo. Il debole ma costante fruscio ritmico dei remi che si avvicinavano. Ascoltammo per essere sicure, per accertarci che le nostre orecchie non ci stessero ingannando. Ma lo sciabordio dei remi diventava sempre più forte. Le nostre voci esplosero di gioia dalla spiaggia fino alla scogliera. Ognuna gridava il nome del proprio amato: Matteo! Francesco! Luigi! Enzo! Filippo! Tutti i nomi esplosero nell'aria. Le nostre voci si sovrapponevano, si scontravano l'una con l'altra. I bambini correvano lungo il bordo dell'acqua, saltando, agitando le braccia, gridando, la loro eccitazione visibile alla luce dei nostri fuochi. Sentii le voci forti di Francesca e Anna, «Papà! Papà! Papà!» Poi cominciammo tutti a gridare. All'improvviso una babele di urla si levò, «Evviva! Sì! Grazie Madre Maria! Eccoli! Ce l'hanno fatta! Mille grazie Santa Rosalia! Alleluia! Oh Mio Dio, grazie!»

Finalmente, i nostri uomini apparvero. Attraverso le fiamme che s'innalzavano davanti a noi, li vedemmo avvicinarsi sempre di più. Con il corpo teso, avanti, indietro, avanti ancora — la forza delle braccia che affondavano e sollevavano i remi dall'acqua — si facevano strada tra le onde impetuose dell'oceano che si aprivano al loro passaggio, tornando a casa. Sempre più vicini. Ancora più vicini. Alla luce della nostra grande fiamma, li vedemmo. Vedemmo le barche da pesca. Vedemmo i nostri mariti, padri, figli, fratelli e zii. Io vidi il mio Matteo.

«Evviva!» Grida Carlo, «Sono tutti salvi!»

«Te l'avevo detto che era la parte più bella,» disse Rosa, «e Nonna Betta, sei stata così intelligente a pensare ad un piano, e anche tutte le altre donne che hanno aiutato gli uomini a tornare a casa, vero?»

«Sì, siamo state intelligenti, e siamo state tutte molto coraggiose.»

«Nonna, tu avevi paura, e hai comunque aiutato i pescatori,» disse Carlo. «Anche la mia mamma aveva paura?»

Francesca si girò dal fornello, dove stava cuocendo qualcosa, e disse, «Carlo, ero una bambina. All'inizio avevo paura, ma Nonna Betta e tutte le donne furono così forti che si presero cura anche di noi. Si assicurarono che fossimo al sicuro. E Giovanni, tuo zio, rimase tutto il tempo con me, con tuo zio Domenico, mia cugina Anna e i nostri Nonni, i tuoi bisnonni. Non ci lasciò mai. Nonna sapeva di potersi fidare di lui per proteggerci.»

«Wow, Nonna,» disse Carlo, «sono contento di non esserci stato. So che mi sarei spaventato davvero.»

«Sono sicura che saresti stato un bambino coraggioso.» Sorridendo ai miei nipoti, sussurrai, «Oh, guarda, Alessandro si è addormentato. Finiremo la storia e poi faremo la festa per il Nonno Matteo.»

La giornata era finita. La grande nube nera era sparita. La calma era tornata. L'intero paese riposava nella sicurezza delle sue famiglie, nelle loro case, rannicchiati nel tepore dei letti. Io ero tra le braccia di Matteo mentre mi stringeva forte. Sentivo il suo amore e la sua stanchezza. Mentre si assopiva, lo sentii sussurrare, «Grazie per avermi salvato oggi, Betta. Grazie per aver salvato tutti noi. Grazie per aver salvato il nostro paese. Sei meravigliosa.»

Distesa lì, guardavo fuori dalle grandi porte aperte che davano sul balcone. Non riuscivo a dormire. Pensando alla giornata che avevamo vissuto, il mio corpo tremava al ricordo gelido. Ricordavo i presagi del mattino. Li aveva sentiti anche Matteo, lasciando Giovanni a casa per aiutare con la famiglia? Madonna mia!

Mi alzai piano per non svegliare Matteo o nessun altro in casa. In punta di piedi andai verso le porte. Avevo ancora paura di uscire sul balcone, così guardai fuori, verso l'oceano e in alto. Non restava che l'oscurità della notte, ma era un cielo pieno di speranza, con stelle che brillavano luminose. Un cielo che, ancora una volta, ci univa alle nostre famiglie, ai nostri amici, al nostro villaggio e a Dio e al Suo universo. La luna crescente brillava sopra di noi. Le stelle scintillavano il loro messaggio, guidate dalla stella più luminosa di tutte, «Siete stati saldi nella vostra fede, e siete al sicuro.» Con gratitudine, guardai in direzione della nostra chiesa, la Chiesa di Santa Rosalia. Fu allora che vidi una luce giù nella strada. Era la mia amica Maria sulla soglia di casa?

Avvolsi lo scialle attorno alle spalle e uscii senza fare rumore dalla camera da letto. Passando per la cucina, presi la candela che aveva illuminato la nostra casa nel corso della giornata. Con attenzione, scesi le scale tastando il muro, ancora scossa dagli eventi del giorno ma sollevata che fosse tutto finito. Aprii la porta d'ingresso sulla strada. Vidi Maria, la fiamma della sua candela la illuminava. Poi Grazia e Giulia, Vincenza, Serafina, Antonina, Lucrezia. Presto vidi anche altre persone.

Rimasi sulla soglia, tenendo la mia candela, guardando su per la strada verso la nostra Chiesa di Santa Rosalia. Immaginando quella stella più luminosa che illuminava la croce sacra sulla cima del suo tetto, rivolsi un ringraziamento a lei, la santa patrona della nostra regione, per averci protetti. Alzando lo sguardo al cielo ringraziai Dio e i Santi per aver salvato i nostri uomini. Ringraziai Maria Santissima delle Grazie per aver interceduto per noi e salvato l'intera comunità dalla confusione della giornata. Una ad una, le altre porte si aprivano lungo le case strette, attaccate l'una all'altra, che portavano alla nostra Santa Rosalia. Le famiglie uscivano con la propria luce di ringraziamento.

Le scale scricchiolarono dietro di me, passi attutiti, quattro persone che scendevano lentamente. Stretti l'uno nelle braccia dell'altro, io e Matteo ci ritrovammo con i nostri figli, come una cosa sola. Giuseppa e la sua famiglia si unirono a noi. Il nostro villaggio, i nostri quartieri, le nostre famiglie erano di nuovo insieme.

Il fiume di luci di candele saliva per la strada, riflettendosi sui colori terrosi delle nostre case, illuminando il cammino su per la montagna verso la Chiesa di Santa Rosalia.

All'improvviso le sue campane cominciarono a suonare. Il loro suono musicale si fece sempre più forte, riempiendo le nostre orecchie di gioia. Ristoravano le nostre anime alla fine di un giorno tormentato ma trionfante. Ci cullarono per un'ora intera, avvolgendoci ancora una volta nella sicurezza della nostra fede. Le campane di Santa Rosalia suonarono fino a mezzanotte, quando accolsero il nuovo giorno. Un giorno per ringraziare Dio di aver creato la luce, per averci donato la saggezza di usarla tramite il fuoco, affinché i nostri uomini potessero vederla e tornare a casa; un giorno per ritrovarci ancora una volta nella sicurezza del nostro piccolo paese ai piedi delle nostre montagne.

Mentre restavo lì ad ascoltare le campane della chiesa, di nuovo al sicuro, pensai, «Ricorderemo per sempre questo momento. Trasmetteremo la sua storia ai nostri figli e nipoti. E loro la trasmetteranno ai propri figli e nipoti, di generazione in generazione, così che tra centinaia e centinaia d'anni si saprà ancora che le donne di Terrasini salvarono il loro villaggio di pescatori dal saccheggio dell'oscurità.»

«Grazie, Nonna Betta,» esclama Rosa. «Questa è la mia storia preferita. Prometto che la racconterò ai miei figli e ai miei nipoti.»

Carlo interviene, «Anch'io, anch'io, Nonna. Ora che so come finisce, adoro questa storia.»

Rosa gli dà una spinta e dice, «Sì, Nonna, manterremo viva la tua storia.»

Francesca mi guarda e sorride. Un sorriso pieno di complicità, ricordando quel giorno e commossa dall'entusiasmo di sua figlia nel voler portare avanti la nostra tradizione del raccontare.

Siamo nella nostra cucina al piano terra, nella stessa casa in cui vivevamo quel giorno spaventoso. Nonno Battista e Nonna Giovanna non ci sono più, e ora la casa è nostra. Francesca e la sua famiglia vivono con me. Domenico e la sua famiglia abitano al piano di sopra, eppure Alessandro è sempre qui a giocare con i suoi cugini.

«I dolci sono pronti,» chiama Francesca.

Guardo i bambini mentre corrono a prendere la loro merenda. Il mio cuore è ancora appesantito dal ricordo del pericolo di quel giorno, ma si scalda nei ricordi di Matteo e della nostra famiglia. Sussurro, «Buon Onomastico, Matteo, Buon Onomastico!»

APPENDICE

Questa storia è stata ispirata dalle coraggiose donne di Terrasini, Sicilia, come raccontato in una leggenda tramandata di generazione in generazione. Il 1° settembre 1726, un evento meteorologico straordinario colpì il loro piccolo villaggio, e la leggenda narra del ruolo vitale delle donne nella gestione delle conseguenze di questo evento. Ho avuto la fortuna di ascoltarla direttamente da Vincenza Randazzo.

Ho incontrato Vincenza nel gennaio del 2020, quando era membro dello staff della Biblioteca e Archivio Storico di Terrasini. Con una scrollata di spalle, mi disse, «Nessuno scrive mai delle donne.» La tradizione della narrazione orale è stata il modo in cui lei, e molti altri, hanno preservato queste storie.

Con le parole di Vincenza che riecheggiavano nelle mie orecchie, mi sono sentita ispirata a rendere omaggio alle donne e agli altri abitanti del villaggio che aiutarono a riportare a casa i pescatori quel giorno. Per me, e per molti, tramandare storie attraverso la narrazione è più di un semplice intrattenimento. A volte è l'unica storia che conosciamo delle nostre famiglie e comunità. Sebbene alcuni dettagli possano mancare o debbano ancora essere scoperti, mi sono presa una licenza creativa per raccontare la storia.

Un Evento Meteorologico

Esistono incertezze sui dettagli di questo evento a Terrasini, ma un terremoto colpì la città di Palermo, che si trova nelle vicinanze, il 1° settembre 1726, alle 5.04 del mattino. Seguì un incendio devastante che distrusse il centro, uccise centinaia di persone, abbatté edifici e seminò il panico.

Gli effetti di quel terremoto a Palermo sono probabilmente ciò che colpì anche Terrasini, che potrebbe essere accaduto simultaneamente ma, secondo alcune storie e tradizioni attuali, è anche probabile che si sia trattato di un effetto secondario. La mia storia presuppone che l'incidente sia avvenuto nel pomeriggio.

La Nascita di Nuove Tradizioni

La potente esperienza di questo evento diede origine a una tradizione. La notte di ogni 1° settembre, prima di mezzanotte, le famiglie si radunavano sulle loro porte come avevano fatto quel giorno fatidico. Illuminati dalla luce delle loro candele tremolanti, pregavano in segno di ringraziamento per la loro salvezza e la fuga dal pericolo. Le campane della chiesa riempivano l'aria in modo solenne in memoria dell'evento, fino all'arrivo del nuovo giorno alle allo scoccare della mezzanotte.

Nel 2016, anno del 290° anniversario di questo evento, il comune di Terrasini pubblicò un libro intitolato *A Terrasini il 1 settembre accade che . . .* , un opuscolo che commemorava la tradizione e spiegava la sua storia come raccontata da Salvatore Cascio.

Gli scritti di Salvatore Cascio, un tempo Direttore della Biblioteca, includono estratti dal diario di D. Antonino Mongitore dal 1720 al 1736 e offrono stralci di resoconti che descrivono l'evento del 1° settembre 1726. Racconti successivi, riferiti a Don Raffaele

Speciale nei primi anni del suo servizio presso la parrocchia di Maria SS. delle Grazie e anch'essi inclusi negli scritti di Salvatore Cascio, presentano memorie contraddittorie, rendendo incerto il fenomeno esatto che diede origine a questa tradizione a Terrasini: terremoto, maremoto o nube nera.

Don Raffaele Speciale abbracciò la tradizione del 1° settembre e istituì un programma liturgico per onorarla, poiché, come riportato da Salvatore Cascio, riteneva appropriata una celebrazione spirituale più profonda e significativa. Egli inserì questa commemorazione all'interno della Festa della Madonna delle Grazie, oggi riconosciuta come Patrona di Terrasini, ed è ampiamente accreditata per aver interceduto in favore degli abitanti, salvando il paese in quel fatidico 1° settembre 1726.

Conosciuta come la *Notte delle Luci*, la tradizione delle famiglie che si riuniscono sulla soglia delle loro case, circondate da candele e lanterne, continua ancora oggi e si è ampliata fino a includere le luminose installazioni nella Piazza Duomo, di fronte alla Chiesa di Maria SS. delle Grazie.

Numerosi sono i racconti di eroismo, simili a quello del 1° settembre 1726. Nel secolo scorso, le donne di Terrasini erano solite allinearsi lungo il porto con le candele accese per aiutare i pescatori a tornare sani e salvi a casa. Maria (Mia) Millefoglie, originaria di Gloucester, Massachusetts, e frequente visitatrice di Terrasini, apprese da una cugina siciliana la storia di un episodio avvenuto negli anni '30: il suo bisnonno, Antonio Millefoglie, fu sorpreso da una tempesta in mare, mentre la sua bisnonna, Antonia Cracchiolo, era tra le donne che nel porto tenevano in mano una grande candela a colonna. Secondo il racconto, le donne portarono con loro anche un ritratto incorniciato della Madonna, un dipinto che oggi è esposto nella Chiesa di Maria SS. della Provvidenza.

La Famiglia di Betta e Matteo

I nomi dei membri della famiglia descritti in questa storia sono reali. Nel 1726, Paola Elisabetta L'Abbate (chiamata *Betta* in questa storia) e la sua famiglia vivevano a Cinisi. (Cinisi comprendeva Favarotta, il villaggio di pescatori che in seguito conosciuto come Terrasini). La famiglia era composta da Paola, il marito Matteo Palazzolo e i loro tre figli: Giovanni, Domenico e Francesca; dal fratello di Matteo, Francesco Palazzolo assieme alla moglie Antonina Giuseppa Cavataio e loro figlia Anna; e dai genitori di Matteo e Francesco, Giambattista Palazzolo e Giovanna Giordano. Giambattista e Giovanna avevano altri figli, ma non compaiono in questa storia. Rosa, Carlo e Alessandro erano i nipoti di Paola. Poiché oggi le informazioni sulle genealogie di secoli fa non possono sempre essere prese alla lettera, nella storia Rosa viene descritta come una bambina di 6 anni, Carlo di 5 anni e Alessandro di 2 anni.

La Famiglia di Betta e il legame con Gloucester, Massachusetts, USA

Grazie all'abbondanza di pesce lungo la costa di Terrasini, nel XVII secolo numerosi pescatori iniziarono a stabilirsi nella zona. Sebbene non sia chiaro esattamente quando la famiglia di Paola Elisabetta (*Betta*) L'Abbate abbia iniziato a dedicarsi alla pesca, è noto che diverse generazioni di pescatori della sua famiglia vissero a Terrasini prima di emigrare a Gloucester nei primi anni del 1900.

Le informazioni sulla famiglia di Paola si basano sulle ricerche genealogiche di Grace Parisi McArdle. La madre di Grace, Mary Josephine Scola Parisi, e Madeline Scola Ventimiglia erano cugine di primo grado e vivevano a Gloucester. Madeline era la nonna di Francis Joseph Ventimiglia, mio marito. Queste famiglie Scola discendono da Sebastiano Scola e Maria Crocifissa (Josephine) Brancaleone Scola, una delle prime famiglie di immigrati italiani a stabilirsi a Gloucester. Paola e la sua famiglia sono antenati di Maria Crocifissa (Josephine) Brancaleone. Con il generoso permesso di Grace, ho utilizzato questi personaggi nel mio libro Le Donne della Luce: La Storia di Betta, ambientato nel quartiere in cui vissero gli antenati Scola nel 1800 a Terrasini, e nella loro chiesa, la Chiesa di Santa Rosalia, con l'attuale piazzetta.

Offerte Votive

Il modellino della barca di Matteo è conosciuto come offerta votiva o ex-voto. Le offerte votive esprimono devozione o gratitudine a Dio o a un santo per aver interceduto in favore di un fedele, in ringraziamento per una preghiera esaudita, un miracolo ricevuto o in attesa di una grazia futura. Gli ex-voto possono assumere molte forme, ma una delle più comuni è l'accensione delle candele votive nelle chiese. In molte chiese costiere, inoltre, le barche o le navi vengono offerte come ex-voto per chiedere protezione per una persona cara in mare.

A Terrasini, gli esempi più evidenti di ex-voto presenti oggi nelle chiese sono le candele votive. Tuttavia, le altre forme di offerte votive, cariche di significato, si inseriscono perfettamente nella storia e offrono uno sguardo più profondo sulla devozione del villaggio.

La Statua di San Pietro

Una statua di San Pietro, patrono dei pescatori, si trova oggi in una nicchia nella Chiesa di Maria SS. della Provvidenza, conosciuta come la chiesa dei pescatori, costruita in un'epoca successiva a quella del racconto. Tuttavia, nella Storia di Betta, la statua è descritta come situata nella Chiesa di Santa Rosalia e raffigurata mentre tiene in mano offerte votive a forma di barche da pesca.

Lucerne

Seguendo i gesti delle mani che Vincenza Randazzo usò mentre descriveva la scena sulla spiaggia, ho immaginato un recipiente che potesse essere facilmente tenuto, racchiuso nel palmo di una mano. Una ricerca sulle possibili opzioni mi ha portato alla lucerna coperta in terracotta, una lampada che all'epoca potrebbe essere stata usata per illuminare le case.

Le Campane di Santa Rosalia

È probabile, che quel giorno siano state le campane della Chiesa di Santa Rosalia a risuonare. Oggi a Terrasini ci sono numerose chiese, ma solo la Chiesa di Santa Rosalia, costruita alla fine del XVII secolo, aveva un campanile nel 1726. La Chiesa Madre, Maria SS. delle Grazie, fu costruita nel 1713 sul sito di una piccola cappella edificata inizialmente nel 1683, ma i suoi campanili furono aggiunti solo molto più tardi, nel 1908. La Chiesa di Maria SS. della Provvidenza fu costruita nel 1923, anch'essa partendo da una piccola cappella, e fu istituita come parrocchia autonoma nel 1953. Altre chiese e cappelle adornano la splendida cittadina di Terrasini, una comunità ancora oggi profondamente radicata nella sua fede.

RINGRAZIAMENTI

Come può davvero una scrittrice iniziare a ringraziare a fondo coloro che hanno contribuito a dare vita ad un'idea di storia? Poche parole su una pagina sembrano non bastare, quindi a tutti voi, sappiate che la mia gratitudine sincera va ben oltre qualsiasi sentimento espresso qui. Grazie. Mille grazie a tutti.

Il sogno che ha ispirato questo racconto è stato accolto da Vincenza Randazzo, una donna vivace, impegnata nella conservazione delle storie locali siciliane e nel riconnettere le persone alle loro famiglie, ai loro antenati e al loro patrimonio culturale siciliano.

Quando il sogno si è presentato, io ero lì, lo stavo vivendo. Ho sentito il legame della famiglia, così mi sono rivolta agli antenati terrasinesi di mio marito per trovare i nomi, per dare un volto alla famiglia che, nel mio sogno, aveva vissuto quel giorno di settembre del 1726. L'incredibile ricerca genealogica di Grace

Parisi McArdle, originaria di Gloucester, ha reso possibile personalizzare questa storia ed il suo significato.

L'incoraggiamento a scrivere questa storia e la fiducia che potessi riuscirci sono arrivati, con particolare entusiasmo, da Wayne Soini. Appassionato di storia e autore di oltre 30 libri, è sempre pronto a sostenere ogni collega scrittore che incrocia il suo cammino, e con me ha dimostrato anche una grande pazienza.

Scrivere può essere un viaggio solitario, ma condividere il proprio lavoro con altri colleghi offre un ambiente di supporto e un prezioso riscontro costruttivo, che ho avuto la fortuna di ricevere dal mio gruppo di scrittura, in particolare da Danuta, George, Lise, Bill, Dan, Susan e Wayne.

Ricostruire le sfumature di una vita vissuta nel contesto di un'epoca storica è sempre una sfida. Per questa storia, l'aiuto di Maria (Mia) Millefoglie è stato preziosissimo.

La versione finale di questo racconto non sarebbe così ricca senza la comprensione, i commenti e i suggerimenti di questi lettori: Grace Ventimiglia Simpson, Beth Simpson, Wayne Soini, Laura Jones Ventimiglia, Arwen Severance, Lynn Clarkson e Diletta Ballati.

Naturalmente, ogni autore ha bisogno di un team di produzione. Terry Weber Mangos si è rivelata l'editor perfetta: ha veramente rispettato la storia, ha onorato la mia voce e ha mostrato una dedizione costante in ogni fase del processo di pubblicazione. Camille Vicenti, una talentuosa e raffinata graphic designer, ha dimostrato lo stesso impegno nello sviluppo del libro. Insieme, i loro talenti hanno contribuito ad una pubblicazione di qualità.

Allie Nicastro, un'illustratrice i cui antenati emigrarono da Terrasini a Gloucester, è stata una collaboratrice vivace e creativa.

Diletta Ballati e Alicia Ballati, originarie dell'Italia settentrionale ma perfettamente a loro agio sia a Gloucester che a Terrasini, hanno offerto con entusiasmo i loro servizi di traduzione, il loro incoraggiamento, l'amore per la storia familiare e per il patrimonio italiano che condividiamo. Diletta, che ha collaborato come lettrice e traduttrice della *Storia di Betta*, è la mia partner in tutti i progetti legati all'Italia, e Alicia era con me quel giorno nel gennaio 2020, ad ascoltare Vincenza mentre raccontava la leggenda.

Infine, la mia famiglia e mio marito, Frank Ventimiglia, hanno sempre creduto in me e mi hanno sostenuto nel seguire i miei sogni.

ITALIAN GLOSSARY

Andiamo – Let's go
basta – Enough
Buon giorno – Good morning
Buon onomastico – Happy name day
Buona domenica – Happy Sunday
Cara/Caro – Dear
Cassateddi di Ricotta – fried sweet ricotta turnovers
È stata una bella giornata – It was a beautiful day
Gesù – Jesus
Giuggiulena – Sicilian sesame seed cookies
Grazie – thank you
Grazie mille – a thousand thanks
i faraglioni – the sea stacks, rock formations in coastal waters
la Chiesa di Santa Rosalia – The church of Saint Rosalia
la Torre Mulinazzo – the tower built in the late 1500s on land jutting into the waters off Terrasini and Cinisi
lucerna/lucerne – oil lamp/s

Madonna del Rosario – Our Lady of the Rosary
Madonna mia – Oh my goodness (similar to 'Oh My God' but often with a stronger emotion or emphasis)
Madre Maria – Mother Mary
Maria Santissima delle Grazie –
Blessed Mother Mary of Graces (Standard Italian translation)
Our Lady of Grace (the church's translation)
Holy Mother of Grace (a conversational translation)
Niente – nothing
Nonna – grandmother
Nonni – grandparents
Nonno – grandfather
ocra gialla – yellow ocher, a natural earthen pigment commonly found in Italy
Oh Mio Dio – Oh My God
onomastico – name day, Saint's Day. The feast day of a Saint when Italians celebrate the baptismal name of a person associated with that Saint
Papà – Daddy
pasta con le sarde – pasta with sardines
Per favore – Please

Piazza Duomo – Cathedral Square, the main square in a town or city which is the location of the Mother Church

piazzetta – small square, *piazza*

prega per – Pray for (*noi* – us, *i nostri uomini* – our men, *nostro paese* – our village)

San Pietro – Saint Peter

Santa – holy or saint

Santa Rosalia – Saint Rosalia

Scirocco – the hot dusty winds that come from the deserts of Libya that can occur anytime during the year although most frequently in the spring and late fall

Sei meravigliosa – You are wonderful

Tutte le donne – All the women

un riposo – a rest

una torta di marzapane – a marzipan cake

Va bene – Okay

Va tutto bene – All is well

Venite qui – Come here